DOG DAYS OF VOODOO

A MALVEAUX CURSE MYSTERY (BOOK 1)

G.A. CHASE

BAYOU MOON PRESS, LLC

Copyright © 2017 by G.A. Chase
First Edition 2017
Cover Art by Janet Holmes
Editing by Red Adept
ISBN eBook: 978-1-940299-40-2
ISBN Print: 978-1-940299-41-9

Bayou Moon Press, LLC

DOG DAYS OF VOODOO

Absolutely nothing stands between a woman and her beloved dog... not even the malevolent force of a voodoo curse.

Kendell Summer, lead guitarist for Polly Urethane and the Strippers, has always been interested in the unexplained. So when she sets off on a paranormal research romp with Myles, a former classmate, to explore his skills in psychometry, she's ready for a little adventure. But she gets more than she bargained for when her Lhasa apso, Cheesecake, is dognapped. Kendell will do whatever it takes to get her dog back.

While rescuing the pup, Kendell and Myles learn that the touristy glitz of New Orleans' voodoo shops hides a dark history few understand—a truth that some in the city plan to use for their own gain.

Soon they uncover more than they ever wanted to know about New Orleans' unsavory past and a curse that threatens to change everything. Only Kendell can prevent the evil they've uncovered from doing more damage, but she'll need Myles's support and psychometric abilities—and the vigilance of the ever-watchful Cheesecake.

The World War II fighter plane crashed into the dark emerald-green water of the Gulf of Mexico, dislodging its overhead canopy. The heavy glass dome shifted and snapped back down, trapping the pilot's arms in the narrow cockpit. Desperation set in fast as he yanked his body against the restraining harness. Water flowed over the instruments' gauges like a menacing waterfall.

"Move, goddammit!" His words echoed around the diminishing air pocket in the cockpit, but his arms remained frozen in place. His hands still gripped the joystick as if he could fly the plane in water as easily as in the sky.

Frantic, he tried pulling his arms from under the displaced glass dome that had been designed to protect him but was now the bear trap that prevented his escape. It was no use. The metal lip that cut deep into his flesh had crushed the bones in both arms.

"Fuck!" His training argued a pilot never gave up hope, but panic had a way of supplanting logic. What breaths he could take came with painful jabs to his chest. Either his ribs had been crushed or he was having a heart attack brought on by fear. He prayed for heart failure over drowning.

As the icy water filled the small compartment, blood from the wounds on his arms sent black eddies into the water illuminated by the meaningless gauges. He turned from the scene of his body being consumed by the gulf waters and sought rescue from some unknown source beyond the sinking plane. All he saw was the angled wing of his fighter dip down as if preparing for a strafing run against some enemy of the deep. His harness held him firmly against the seat.

There was no escape.

Once filled with the ocean's salt water, the craft dove sharply below the waves. His eyes were still protected by his goggles and were the last of his senses to function correctly. Having exhausted every option for escape, he closed his eyes, choosing the undistorted view of the murky depths as the final scene to his life. With no fight left in him, the warrior gave in to the inevitable. The blackness of the deep separated his consciousness from the hell around him.

Myles Garrison woke in a cold panic. His hands grasped his arms, certain he'd be clutching the torn leather airman's jacket. Instead, he felt the sting of a growing sunburn on his unprotected chest. "Swing the boat around."

He felt the powerful vibration of the inboard engine starting up against his back as he lay on the front fiberglass deck of the dive boat *Sea Conch*. The sensation brought him to full consciousness. A disgruntled voice rang down from the wheelhouse. "What now?"

"I want to dive. Right over there."

The voice came across muffled as the captain turned away from Myles. "Please go talk to him. We're less than an hour from the oil rig. There's good diving out there, lots of sea life. I only agreed to stop so y'all could take a dip to cool off."

Vanesa, in her skimpy dive bikini, worked her way along the polished-chrome rail to the front of the boat. "You were asleep."

"No. I wasn't. This is where I want to dive." He knew his companions' impression of him. They hadn't even bothered to hide their irritation. He didn't care. This was his expedition. He'd paid for the charter. And they'd dive where he wanted. "There's a World War II airplane down there. I want to see it."

Water dripped off her long, bare legs as she stood over him with her arms crossed. "Trust me. You were asleep. I could hear you snoring."

"You were sitting on the back of the boat, and you heard me snoring all the way up here? I wasn't asleep. I saw the crash."

She moved her hands from her elbows to her hips as she looked at the sky. "Charlie is going to have a fit. We've only enough daylight for one more good dive, and you want to waste it out here?"

"I'm telling you I saw the plane. It's down there."

Her tanned body, barely covered by the light-blue

neoprene fabric, was more compelling than her argument. "Yeah? You mean like yesterday when you thought you were a pirate captain? We spent half the day poking around in those sandbars. All I saw was one crab."

"It was a pretty piraty-looking crab." Myles turned to see Charlie leaning against the cabin.

Vanesa was a hard person to impress. "Yeah, a regular reincarnation of Jean Laffite. But other than some random shells, he didn't seem forthcoming about his buried treasure."

Myles struggled to his feet while trying not to slip on the smooth fiberglass. "I know you think I'm nuts. But you did agree to come out here with me. I promise if there's nothing down there, we can spend all day tomorrow diving wherever you want."

Charlie scowled as he nodded. "I suppose we did agree to help you with this quest to prove your insanity. But whether we find something or not, the drinks are on you tonight."

Myles stared out at the featureless water, hoping he wasn't once again wrong about his abilities. At least there would only be a couple of people laughing at him this time. Finding people who might be open-minded enough to join him on his adventures was becoming a challenge.

~

THE EARLY-AUTUMN SUN lit up Kendell Summer's small kitchen. Her hand didn't move from the coffee cup on her small dining table as she reread the article in the

Southeastern Louisiana State alumni paper. She couldn't have cared less about the picture of the restored airplane that had been used in place of the actual discovery or even the explanation of how it was found. She knew a bullshit story when she read one. If all treasure hunters had to do was study sonar readings and underwater charts, there'd be a lot more crap dredged up from the ocean's depths. But the goofy, smiling face on the guy standing next to the attractive, serious couple rang a bell. She'd shared a class with him. He too had fallen for the shyster's advertisement for a made-up college course.

The class had been one of her dumber mistakes as a music student. How was she to know The Transfer of Human Energy into Inanimate Objects wasn't sanctioned by the state college? She had reasoned that just because it wasn't listed in the course catalogue didn't mean it wasn't a valid class. With all of the institutions of higher learning in New Orleans, nearly anything someone wanted to teach was validated by some organization. She should have known better. Nothing she believed in her soul ended up being true.

The study of how intensely emotional events left a record in those things around the person matched up nicely with how she viewed her beloved guitar. Every sad moment as a pre-teen strumming out songs on the instrument had mellowed its sound like the yellowing of the varnish on the white-spruce wood top. Now in her twenties, she could play everything from classical music to David Bowie on the old guitar—and tap into emotional depths impossible to find in even the most expensive of instruments. Her parents had emphasized that *love* wasn't a term to be used for things. But Cecile, Kendell's guitar, understood her better than any person ever would. After a lifetime of being told physical objects didn't carry emotions, she'd finally found a professor who believed they did. If only such fantasies had any basis in reality.

Now this Myles doofus seemed to have broken the code of how to turn theory into reality.

Kendell slapped the paper to the table and looked at her overweight Lhasa apso basking in the morning sun on her beloved ottoman. "Cheesecake, I'm going to call him."

She never lied to her dog. Telling her eleven-year companion of her plans was as good as chiseling them in stone.

The dog looked up at her with sleepy brown eyes. The idea wasn't the dumbest one Kendell had ever told her about.

"I promise I won't let my imagination carry me away. I just want to find out if this guy's discovered something interesting. Don't look so worried. I expect to be let down this time."

∽

MYLES SAT in the funky coffee shop lined with books. Frenchmen Street wasn't one of his usual New Orleans hangouts. There were too many hipster types lounging around trying to look intellectual.

He gave up trying to place the small, spunky girl behind the counter who greeted everyone with a smile. She'd said on the phone that her name was Kendell Summer. Apparently, they'd gone to college together. There was a cute girl-next-door quality to her interactions, but as she wasn't six feet tall with blond hair that reached all the way to her butt, he couldn't be expected to remember her.

His lack of recognition wasn't a complete surprise. He viewed his school years as a marathon, and college had been the last lap. Those students around him were not competitors as much as obstacles threatening to trip him up. Women particularly fit that description. Each night, he suffered the dilemma of whether to study or go drinking with his friends in the bars that lined Bourbon Street. Women and alcohol had waylaid more than one fellow student in his class. It took all of his time and energy to pass the courses on dead civilizations. Archeology was supposed to be about getting outside and playing in the dirt, not getting buried under books so boring they sucked the life out of him.

She set two steaming mugs of coffee on the table and took off her apron. The café was trying to be too homey for his tastes. Paper cups held more and would let him take the drink and go if the conversation got boring. Actual mugs were a not-so-subtle way of keeping the customer in the shop.

"Thanks for meeting me." Her voice had a soft, calming tone that reminded him of a woman singing a lullaby.

"No problem. I work in the Quarter as a bartender, so this is on my way." He had to admire any woman brave enough to make the first move even if she wasn't his type. He must have made quite the impression on her in college.

Her short hair was as black as her coffee. "I have to confess I didn't remember you when I first read the article in the alumni paper."

Now he was confused, which was not an unusual situation for him when it came to women. "Then why did you make contact?"

"Do you remember that off-campus class on energy transfer?"

Myles closed his eyes in horror. She was one of those whack jobs who believed in the supernatural. She probably belonged to some coven. Now that he thought about it, she did look a little like a sexy witch. "We all make mistakes."

She leaned forward over her coffee. "But you did it, didn't you? You figured it out. How to read energy that had been left behind in an object. You really did it." The steam rising to her face only reinforced his image of her as a witch.

"You've got the wrong idea. I didn't take that stupid class looking for answers. I make up stories, okay? Ever since I was a little kid, I'd pick up some rock and imagine it was thrown into my yard by an Indian chief hundreds of years ago. My parents said I had a hyperactive imagination. I had some time to kill, my junior year, and thought that class might be a good way to refine my debate skills. Any teacher willing to stand in front of a class and expound nonsense about physical objects being recording devices deserved whatever arguments he got. Seeing as how I understood where he was coming from, I thought sparring with him might be a useful exercise."

Kendell's brown eyes looked so large and trusting he felt

bad about laying into her like that. "Then what were you doing looking for that plane?"

"Just because my parents thought I had an overactive imagination didn't mean I had to listen to them. Conducting quiet private research is vastly different from standing in front of a bunch of students talking out your ass." He put his coffee cup down as a waitress stopped by to refill it. "I've always been lucky at finding things—lost keys, wallets, you name it. When I go camping, I seem to run across all the garbage that's left behind. I sometimes find junk that's been sitting there in the dirt for a hundred years. But that's all it is—luck."

"Finding that plane didn't sound like luck."

He settled back in the overstuffed lounge chair, wondering how much he should trust her. Even his friends thought his ideas were crazy. "That professor thought emotions were like sound waves. As they hit the atoms of an object, they could affect how they vibrated. Kind of like a tape player."

"I remember an argument you had with him about the saying *if these walls could talk*. It got pretty heated."

Myles took the small porcelain pitcher of cream and poured some in his coffee. "There's a theory in physics that says it's impossible for me to completely mix this milk into my coffee. If I could get down to the submolecular level, I could still reverse the flow and turn it back into two liquids. But it's all theory. I couldn't actually take this spoon and unmix what I've done. To hear the voices in the walls would be like unmixing my coffee. Plus, every person who ever visited the room would be affecting the molecular movement. It'd just be a jumble."

"You do a remarkably good job of explaining why what you did didn't work. After all, you did find that airplane."

Myles shrugged. "I'm just explaining why that class was bullshit."

"Then tell me what isn't bullshit. Because that's what excites me."

For the first time, he looked at her with interest. "Me too. That's what I'm trying to figure out."

The sexy-nerd look wasn't one he responded to, but it worked well on her. "If you can't explain what you did, could you show me?"

No one had ever asked for a demonstration. He felt a little like she'd just asked to watch him masturbate. "I'm not sure how that would work."

"We could take it on as a scientific experiment. First, we'd have to find an object for you to read."

In their short conversation, she'd shown more interest in his process than anyone he could remember. "Where do you propose we find such a thing?"

2

_____

Of all the streets in the French Quarter, Royal was Myles's least favorite. It was lined with high-end antique stores displaying price tags so high it'd take him a year's salary to buy an end table. Locals who worked in the service industry didn't frequent the area. "There's a lot of old stuff in these shops, but I doubt they're going to let us touch anything."

"I didn't bring you down here for these rip-off artists. Anyone rich enough to set foot in one of these places deserves to lose their money, or they'd better be damn good at negotiations." She pointed toward a storefront that probably hadn't been cleaned in a decade. "I know it doesn't look like much, but I've found some cool old military hats and jackets in there."

The store specializing in vintage firearms wasn't Myles's idea of an enjoyable place to shop. Guns might have a certain mechanical charm, but he knew he had to be one of the only people in the South who didn't care for the deadly weapons.

As he entered the dusty shop, his skin bristled as though every hair had just stood on end. The high-pitched buzzing in his ears made him wish for the loud earworm '80s songs that were blasted at him every night from the stage as he tended bar. "Can we please get out of here? This place is going to give me a headache."

The excitement on Kendell's face didn't help his disposition. "Are you feeling energy from these weapons? I thought you might. Something in here must have been used for its intended purpose."

She might have had a point, but his discomfort could have just as easily been caused by the fluorescent tube lights that lined the ceiling. "I'm giving this shop five minutes. Then I'm out the door. I don't like guns."

She nodded toward a corner at the back of the shop filled with military uniforms. "Go check over there. They keep the guns and swords up here. If I find something interesting, I'll bring it to you. I suspect you're getting overloaded with past energy. It must be like all these voices are screaming at you all at once."

For someone who was just learning about how energy affected him, she was remarkably perceptive. Most of the heavy field jackets that filled the racks looked to be either reproductions or military overstock. The more expensive uniforms were displayed in nice glass cabinets. He tried on a large navy-blue British peacoat. He doubted the heavy-weather jacket would see more than a day or two's service during a typical New Orleans winter. Even so, being surrounded by so much wool gave him a feeling of protection from the irritating energy that filled the shop.

"What about this one?" Kendell hauled over an old flintlock from a rack beside the door. Based on the metal's patina, the weapon looked like it hadn't been fired since before their grandparents were born. The barrel had to be nearly as long as she was tall.

"You're kidding, right?" He still didn't know what he was doing with the mousy girl in the vintage overcoat. Her large eyes, which peered at him from under her bangs, reminded him of a friend's kid sister.

She shrugged and took it back to the rack. "From your discovery, I thought something older might be easier for you to read. Like the energy had a chance to settle into the molecules or something."

He looked over at the clerk, who shook his head as if he'd heard it all before. Some topics of conversation should really be held in private or at least in whispered tones. How did she not know that?

Losing the peacoat made him feel ten pounds lighter. Between the weight and the heat, in another couple of minutes his body would have been in full sweaty workout mode. The familiar raised hairs on his arm, however, left him to wonder how the heavy garment had managed to suppress the swirling energy of the shop.

He picked up an army knife from the counter. The blade was pitted and dull. It carried no emotion he could detect. If it had killed someone, the soldier wielding the blade must have had some mad stealthy skills for the victim to not have noticed. He thought it more likely that the blade had aged from lack of use.

Kendell snuck up behind him to look around his shoulder into the display case with the cracked glass top. "What's that metal thing with the sculpture of a man's head?"

Myles began forming his arguments for why this outing had been a mistake. Kendell's passion for psychometry—she'd remembered the term from class—was unmistakable. But lumping him in with the fortune-tellers around Jackson Square didn't seem like taking him seriously. He closed his eyes to the childhood memories of being told to stop making stuff up.

He was working on an excuse to leave the shop when the clerk pulled out the ornately carved metal tube. The salesman unscrewed the head and released a small knife blade and reamer. "This is a tobacco-pipe tool. Most of them are pretty plain, but as you can see, this one must have belonged to someone important. Not many people bothered to have one custom made like this. Whoever owned it was probably pretty well off. It came in yesterday with a collection of stuff from the War Between the States. I only put it out because of the knife blade. If you want it, I can let you have it at a good price. There's some Napoleonic daggers coming in next week, so we'll need the display space."

As Myles inspected the head with the attached thin knife blade, Kendell played with the gold cylinder. "It's heavy."

The clerk pointed at the stubby end. "That side is used to tamp the tobacco down into the pipe bowl."

Myles was grateful she'd found someone else to talk to so he could inspect the object in peace. The delicate tool in his hand began to make him feel dizzy. The last thing he wanted to do was explain every passing moment of nausea. The blade slipped out of his hand. He barely had time to slide his foot out of the way of the sharp point, which ended up stuck firmly into the old wood floor.

The clerk raced around the counter. "It didn't get you, did it? That damn thing is bad luck. When we were unloading the packing box, it fell out and cracked the glass display case."

"I'm fine." Myles felt an instant relief to not be handling the object anymore. The clerk had to give the knife a good tug to get it out of the floor.

"Did you feel something?" Kendell's hand was on his waist, helping him maintain his balance.

To his surprise, he did. He knew the delicate knife had tasted blood before. Though with the activity of the French Quarter outside, he couldn't tell very much about the small, seemingly harmless item. "I don't think it likes me very much."

"Who does?" She turned to the clerk. "I'll take it."

~

THEY SAT on the steps of Saint Louis Cathedral, watching a busker entertain the audience with his idea of an erotic puppet show. "You were pretty fast on buying that knife. I'm not even sure I sensed anything worth pursuing."

The fact that she was watching the man in the tight

bodysuit made Myles uncomfortable. The performer's outfit wasn't leaving anything to the imagination, and the way he interacted with his dolls crossed the line from entertaining into creepy. She didn't seem to mind, though. "I could tell you felt something. You'd already said you didn't want to be in that shop any longer than necessary. Plus, I need a gift for my father's birthday. If nothing comes from our little experiment, I'll give it to him."

"Your dad smokes a pipe?"

She pulled out a five-dollar bill and handed it to the marionette dangling in front of the performer's crotch. "No, but he digs weird old shit. It'll look good on his desk."

The doll's head turned expectantly toward Myles. He didn't engage. Fortunately, the busker moved on to more generous members of the audience. "Still seems like an impulsive purchase. Where do we go from here?"

"I think for scientific reasons it'd be better if we limit how much interaction you have with this tool. I also want to be around when you do your thing. You made it sound like you were nearly asleep when you saw the airplane, though there were other people present. I don't know how I could help, but we're in this together."

He could see her logic. They'd need a controlled environment for him to test his ability to read the energy. "I'm not working tonight. I could come by if you're not busy."

He hoped inviting himself over would be seen as less forward then inviting her to his place. Plus, his room in the run-down building that had been built as slaves' quarters didn't impress many women.

"I can't do it tonight. I've got a gig."

A 'gig' in New Orleans could mean damn near anything. "What kind of gig?"

Her smirk made him feel foolish for asking. "I was a music major. What kind of gig do you think?"

He had trouble imagining her on stage. "What type of music do you play?"

"I'm part of an authentic blues-punk band, Polly Urethane and the Strippers. My stage name is Olympia Stain."

There were more questions inspired by those two sentences than he could wrap his head around. "You realize I'm going to have to come see you play."

"Well, we're playing at the Scratchy Dog on Frenchmen Street tonight if you want to broaden your musical experience."

Tending bar on Bourbon Street meant he spent most of his nights enduring '80s' cover bands. A certain amount of punk often seeped in, though it was seldom what the drunk tourists wanted to hear. "I'm not musically naïve. I do know blues-punk. I grew up listening to the White Stripes and the Oblivions. But what is *authentic* blues-punk?"

"It's a genre we made up ourselves. Have you ever heard Devo's cover of the Rolling Stones' 'Satisfaction'? It's kind of like that except we use old blues ballads. You'll have to stick around for our version of Billy Holiday's 'Summertime.' It's my favorite."

The confusing array of mental images that Kendell had presented forced Myles to stare at her for an uncomfortably long time. "I'll be there."

~

THE MUSICAL ESTABLISHMENTS on Frenchmen Street prided themselves on being truer to the jazz culture of New Orleans than those on Bourbon Street. Myles suspected that was truer before the area was overrun with short-term rentals. The clubs maintained their individuality, but increasingly, the patrons weren't much different than the drunks he served. People wanted what they wanted, and even the bohemian clubs had to compete for customers.

The Scratchy Dog was one of the last in the line of well-known music venues. Instead of taking itself seriously and vying for the hipster crowd like all the rest, however, the owner opted for a more tongue-in-cheek niche establishment. Myles slipped Tick, the doorman, ten bucks for a seat up front.

The barmaid brought Myles his Abita Turbo Dog beer. He wondered if he'd just made a terrible mistake as five women in dark glasses and trench coats took the stage, looking like some kind of feminist hit squad.

The curly-haired blonde in the middle shed her coat to reveal a short, tight dress and fishnet stockings. "I'm Polly Urethane, and these are my strippers!"

Polly announced each of her bandmates.

"Minerva Wax on drums!" The long-legged brunette next to Polly pulled open her coat, like a burlesque dancer, to reveal ripped jeans and a black tank top.

"Scraper on bass!" The bass player's shaved head enhanced her look of defiance. She separated the sides of her trench coat like a flasher and glared at the crowd.

"Lynn Seed on keyboards!" The spunky-looking Asian woman licked her lips as she danced out of her overcoat.

"And finally, on lead guitar, Olympia Stain!" Myles had to do a double take to be sure it was really Kendell. She was dressed in a black skirt so short he could see the tops of her ripped nylons. He'd never suspected she had curves that would rival a roller coaster.

All five women raised their right fists as Polly declared, "We're Polly Urethane and the Strippers. We'll sand off the paint of your daily lives, reveal your hardwood, and refinish your view of girls' bands everywhere!"

Each woman hustled to her instrument and began beating out "Baby Please Don't Go" in a tempo that made Myles's heart beat a little too fast for comfort. He'd been around enough bands to know the onstage persona was often just another part of the act. The normally reserved Kendell he knew displayed her sexy-vixen character with abandon as she turned loose a storehouse of energy against the strings of her jet-black electric guitar.

Women took to the floor, exhibiting the typical dance moves of sorority girls having a little too much fun. Men weren't far behind as they found the bravery to venture in front of the gender-aggressive musicians. Myles drank his beer, happy for once to be able to sit back and enjoy the show instead of being the one standing behind the bar, responsible for looking after the drunks.

The music had a dark, grinding edge that took a song or two for Myles to appreciate. But once indoctrinated into the band's version of the classic blues numbers, he doubted he'd ever hear the pieces the same. And like the music,

Kendell as Olympia was a persona that once seen couldn't be ignored. The nerdy girl next door hid a powerful sex vixen under the heavy coat she so frequently wore.

At the break, she plopped into the chair next to him. "God, I love playing with those women. In college, all of my professors and fellow students took music so seriously. Here I just get to cut loose and have fun. This is what music should be about, not sheet music and contracts."

"I can see that. How did you end up joining the group?" Though the studious Kendell and the wild Olympia were clearly two sides of the same person, he couldn't figure out how the shy girl from the day before had found her outlet.

From the way she squinted, he thought she was laughing at him again. "Just because I'm not a party girl doesn't mean I'm a recluse. Music fascinates me. That's why I live so close to the clubs. All this high energy is addictive. Every week, I go out and listen to at least one new band and as many old favorites as I can find. One night, I stumbled in here. Polly's a great singer, but she can't play guitar for shit. Really, she needs to just hold a tambourine. That night I auditioned during their break. She had me on stage in ten minutes. That was nearly a year ago."

Music groups had to do what they could to survive. "I don't see anyone hawking CDs by the door. Do you go on tour?"

"Mostly, we just play around town. The biggest vehicle any of us owns is Minerva's old VW bus. It's not the most reliable vehicle. Polly wants to make the group into something more financially viable, but I just want to play for the fun of it. But then, I'm the only one who doesn't use her stage name outside of our gigs. I love being in the band, but it's not my whole life. Being on stage with people lusting after me while I pour myself into the music is damn near a fetish. That kind of sexual energy has to be enjoyed in small doses."

And he'd felt guilty for studying archeology. At least there wasn't a sexual component to digging in the dirt.

Kendell stood as the women started returning to the stage. "Come by my place tomorrow. I'm usually up by late morning. We can start our research."

3

*M*yles had been in his share of women's apartments. He always experienced a unique feeling of acceptance when a woman invited him over. As he looked around Kendell's small one-bedroom above a touristy bead shop on Decatur Street, he had to remind himself he was only there to talk. But some habits were hard to break, such as casually observing a woman's possessions as a means of getting behind the masks she presented to the outside world.

The large windows that led out to the balcony overlooking the old brick museum were free of curtains. She was neither a prude nor a hermit. Either personality type would have sought to close herself off from the world. But her view wasn't of a neighboring apartment. So being open for her was less a matter of exhibitionism than curiosity. The windows reminded him of her eyes—large and open.

She'd left the door to her bedroom open. Typically, he'd interpret the gesture as a woman welcoming him into her boudoir. But in Kendell's case, he assumed it had more to do with letting as much light as possible into the small space. The room was filled with a large bed so billowy she'd look like a small girl in it. She might not be an open book, but she wasn't shy about letting him get to know her.

As he thought about her, a book seemed the most accurate metaphor. That impression was heightened by the bookcases that lined every available section of wall. There weren't many open slots left for new reading material. He doubted he'd read that many books in his whole life. But as he looked at the titles, he eased off his assessment of her as a nerdy intellectual. There were as many books devoted to the paranormal as there were romance novels. She had eclectic tastes. Talking to her would never be boring, provided he could keep up.

Her furniture was old and comfortable, much like the clothes she wore, but none of it was ratty. It was as if she wanted visitors to know she had her own aesthetic. No one would be dictating fashion to her. She made her own way through life, and she wanted others to see it.

He took a seat on the rumpled couch made up of as many colorful, handmade pillows as cushions. His first impression of Kendell's overweight, elderly dog, who watched him from the ottoman, was that she was looking to him for food. She certainly had the intense stare that usually accompanied begging. "I don't have anything for you. Do you want me to pet you?" He reached out to offer his hand.

The dog growled. "I didn't mean to offend—just thought we could be friends."

Kendell returned from the kitchen with two cups of coffee. "Don't mind her. It takes time for Cheesecake to warm up to men."

"Cheesecake?"

Kendell handed him a cup and sat next to him. "It's a silly name, I know. My parents gave her to me for my twelfth birthday. I fell in love with the puppy immediately." She looked over at the dog basking in the morning light of the front window. "Didn't I, my sweet girl?"

"Okay, but why the name?"

She gave him an exasperated look. "I was getting there. From the time I first tasted the dessert, I've been a firm believer that cheesecake is the ultimate in culinary achievements. And for us to be friends, you'll have to agree with me. It's a cake. It's a pie. And it's made out of light-as-a-feather creamy cheese. It's sheer perfection."

"I like chocolate."

From the way she went silent, closed her eyes, and drew her lips into a stern thin line, he suspected she was counting to ten. When she opened her eyes again, he knew he'd made the mistake of the day. "Why are all the men who cross my path chocolate-headed Neanderthals?"

"There's no such thing as chocolate cheesecake?"

She softened slightly. "There is. I can compromise that far. Just don't go cake boy on me, or we're through."

He knew he probably shouldn't poke her, but the target was too tempting to ignore. "But you said yourself one of the wonders of cheesecake is that it's part cake."

"That's the Neanderthal part. Cake is just unevolved."

He sipped his coffee to prevent her from seeing him laugh. "Okay, so you like cheesecake. Why give that name to the dog?"

"I don't *like* cheesecake. At twelve, it was an all-consuming passion. I had dreams of becoming a chef specializing in making the ultimate cheesecakes. So when I met my puppy, my mother asked me the cruelest question I'd ever heard in my life. I cried I was so hurt."

Myles couldn't for the life of him figure out where Kendell was going with her story. "What did she ask?"

"She wanted to know if I loved the dog more than cheesecake. Can you imagine? I grabbed the puppy in my arms and just held her, petted her, and called her Cheesecake. I remember looking into her big brown eyes and promising I'd never, ever have to tell her I loved her more than cheesecake. She'd already know."

Myles looked over at the dog, wondering what Kendell saw in her. Cheesecake's pronounced underbite reminded him of a hairy Darth Vader mask. "Well, she doesn't seem to think much of me, which is unusual for a dog."

"Cheesecake doesn't like to be lumped in with other dogs. She makes up her own mind about people. It takes time for her to get to know someone. Hurt her, piss her off, or worst of all, make her think you're a threat to me, and she'll never forgive you. She won't even let most of my ex-boyfriends into my apartment. She's never bitten anyone, but if I were ever really in danger, I think she would do it to protect me. And she can't be bribed. Why do guys always think they can win females over just by offering us food?

Cheesecake doesn't base her assessment of people on them giving her treats any more than I fall in love because some guy takes me out to dinner. We're both much more complicated than that. Aren't we, girl?"

"I'll keep that in mind." The way Kendell kept talking to the dog as if she were a part of the conversation made Myles uncomfortable. It wasn't that he didn't think animals understood. They most likely did. He just didn't like being in a multispecies conversation. Throughout his life, people had ignored him in favor of what someone else had to say. Being passed over for a silent dog did little to help his self-confidence.

He spun the small pipe tool on the end table like a pencil. Just as when he played with actual writing implements, he knew he was procrastinating.

She snagged the spinning golden cylinder off the table. "Explain to me how you read energy. I don't understand why it is you could experience everything that pilot went through during a crash eighty years ago in a plane one hundred feet underwater, but you can't tell what's going on with this while it's in your hand."

He barely understood himself. "I was in a different mental state. Here, talking with you or standing in that shop with a bunch of people around, makes me very engaged with my surroundings. My brain is working. Out there on the water, I was attempting to be as mentally blank as possible."

"How did you know you weren't just imagining everything?"

He smiled at her politeness. "My friends on the boat

were less diplomatic. They believed I'd been asleep and dreaming the whole scene. Honestly, I know the difference. I have drifted off more often than I've reached a quiet but alert mind-set."

"So it's kind of like meditation?"

He never went in for spiritual crap. "If you accept that professor's idea that information is stored in objects, you could think of what I do as trying to be the blank screen for the movie to project onto. Meditation sounds too much like trying to turn off all the projectors, not just one playing my personal narrative."

"I thought you didn't like that guy."

Myles couldn't remember a single professor he did like. "I'm just not crazy about people talking about stuff when they haven't tried it themselves. Studying all the theory in the world isn't worth a damn if you never put it into practice. I don't remember one useful topic regarding *how* to read energy, only what it might be like."

"Sounds complicated. How do you know when it's your mind making stuff up and when the story is coming from somewhere else?"

He took the small metal cylinder from her. "That's what we have to find out. I need someplace peaceful where I can lie down. The room doesn't have to be completely quiet. In fact, it would better if there were some kind of white noise, like an air conditioner, or something that would prevent me from falling asleep but not be a distraction."

Her laugh made him feel included in her life—he could tell she wasn't laughing at his expense. "A quiet room in an apartment on Decatur? You must be kidding. You could use my bedroom."

Her innocence made him smile. Even a woman he wasn't immediately attracted to would have things in her private sanctuary he'd find difficult to ignore. "The living room couch would be better, provided Cheesecake doesn't mind me in her space."

"That's cool. I have some reading to do on psychometry. From what I gather, it works better if you're holding the item. I'll take Cheesecake and hide out in my bedroom. Would an hour be long enough?"

He'd never given much thought to how long it would take to connect to old energy. "I think it'd be safe to say that if I haven't gotten some message by then, I'll probably be asleep."

"I'll listen for your snoring just in case."

HE HAD to admit that Cheesecake knew her lounging spots. Winter in New Orleans made relaxing in the light of early afternoon a pleasure. Another couple of months, and he would be avoiding any possibility of adding heat to the already stifling day.

But relaxing in a woman's apartment didn't come naturally. Even with his eyes closed, the smell of her lavender-scented soap and pine candles made him think of being a kid, lying out on a grassy field in summer. So much about her reminded him of those carefree days when he was able to be friends with girls without worrying about sexual tension.

His mental image of a summer's day transitioned to an old-fashioned young girl's yellow dress covered in printed, brightly colored flowers.

A person's thoughts didn't accompany the mental movie, much to Myles's disappointment. There was no narrative voice-over giving him insight into what went on in his character's head. He was left with only the intense emotions and, if he was lucky, the person's reaction as it played out in the private theater of his anti-imagination.

A girl's small finger traced the letters engraved on the pipe tool. Instead of the dull, tarnished-gold cylinder he was familiar with, it gleamed so brightly he could make out the delicate inscription: "To My Father. Love, Serephine."

But as her finger covered up the *Love*, he experienced her intense disappointment. Her father had hurt her, but her emotion was more pity than anger.

Myles allowed his perception of the event to rise closer to his own thoughts. The girl's feelings were intense but quiet. Unlike the pilot, whose terror had left crystal-clear images embedded in the cockpit, this child's movie was in the soft light and long shadows so common to New Orleans. To really hear her, Myles would need an even deeper state of calm no matter what she had to tell him.

He let his mind go blank to sink back down to her awareness. A tear had fallen onto her hands, which held the tool, framed by her gossamer-soft blond hair. Whatever her father had done hadn't resulted in her hatred. But *love* was a term she could no longer accept.

Her small porcelain-white thumb swung the blade out

from the other thin implements. Her heart beat so fast Myles could feel his own corresponding blood pressure in his hands and feet. She drew a faint pink line across her wrist with the blade—at least, she'd intended to keep the pressure light.

Myles struggled to remain in the moment with the girl, but struggling was the opposite of remaining calm and blank. He sat up and wiped the sweat from his forehead. The girl's movie wasn't finished.

He propped up the needlepoint pillow so the sun would shine on his face and lay back on the couch. Whatever had happened to the girl had been long ago. It wasn't like he could help her. He could only hear her story.

She wanted to scream, but all that came out was a whimpering, "No." The fear of anyone finding out what she'd done overwhelmed her need for help.

Ruby-red blood flowed across the girl's lily-white wrist. She held her hand up to her face. The thick liquid ran down her arm and onto her father's large leather office chair. In her other small hand, she still held the delicate knife.

The math didn't add up. She wouldn't have had the strength to press the dull knife deep enough into her flesh even if she had meant to. The little pressure she'd applied, and the unlikely gush of blood that followed, led to confusion in both Myles and the girl. The blood stained her cotton dress before seeping into her leggings and continuing to her patent-leather shoes. She arched her foot up, trying to stop the growing stream from hitting the floor. At the first drop that landed on the embroidered carpet, her only emotion was fear of her father's anger at her for messing up his office.

Hazy black dots began rotating around the image in Myles's mind. The girl's emotions were deepening to a maturity he would have expected from someone much older. She laid the tool in the puddle of blood on the chair.

Again, there was a desire to scream. Death, however, was less feared than a life spent as her father's daughter. She didn't view him as evil, but she knew others would. And society's impression of him would taint her as well. Death would free her of the bonds that held her to her father's actions, to his legacy, and to being his daughter. The movie grew so dark he nearly missed the last image of a butterfly hatching out of its cocoon to fly away.

~

MYLES WAS STILL SEARCHING for the hidden inscription when Cheesecake jumped on the couch to repossess her throne. At least she didn't growl at him.

Kendell followed her dog out of her bedroom. "I'm sorry. She doesn't like being cooped up."

"It's okay. I think I've got the answer I was searching for, but you're not going to like it." Women had a soft spot for children. Telling her about the girl's unintended suicide wasn't going to be an enjoyable conversation.

She sat next to him and held Cheesecake in her lap like some demonic teddy bear as he recounted what he'd seen. Each time he said something that made Kendell cringe, the dog started growling like it was somehow his fault for not saving the poor child.

"But you don't think she had meant to cut her wrist?" The question seemed important to Kendell.

It wasn't like his mental movies came with a rewind feature. "The only emotion I experienced was shock at seeing the blood. I don't know what she intended. I don't get to read her thoughts, just feel her emotions. The knife must have been sharper than she'd expected, but a pipe tool wouldn't need to be razor sharp. It seemed like an accident. I don't know how it happened. She must have been in shock. That's the only explanation I can come up with as to why she didn't yell for help. Though at the end of her life, I got a distinct feeling of relief."

Kendell buried her face in Cheesecake's thick, curly black-and-white fur. "And she was mad at her father? I can't imagine how bad he must have felt thinking his daughter had committed suicide with something she'd given him."

"Again, I don't get to know what she was thinking. All I could experience was what she saw and her emotional responses. Even at her young age, she knew her father was not considered a good man. I don't think she was so much mad at him as hurt for what he'd done to others."

She stared into his eyes for so long he finally had to look away. "How much of her emotions affect you?"

Long ago, he'd learned to focus on himself after experiencing someone else's story, be it real or imaginary. "I'll be fine in a couple of hours."

"That's not what I asked."

Again, he felt as though she was prying into his intensely

personal habits. "That girl's suicide, intentional or not, will always be a part of me. I've experienced death before, as with the pilot, but I've never known what it is to take one's own life. Now I do. It would be tempting to say I can isolate the event like reading about it in a book, but that's not accurate. I was there. Intellectually, I know I couldn't stop something that happened so long ago, but that doesn't relieve the guilt of being behind the girl's eyes while it happened."

"And you carry that load every time you read an object's history? How do you survive such a burden?"

Her question was one he'd struggled with since childhood. "I had a choice. Either I could grow cold to those around me, or I could embrace that we all have our issues to deal with. I wish I could tell you it was a one-time decision. The truth is I struggle with that duality every day."

Kendell scratched at the dog's ear as she thought. "So we have an object that we think carries an emotional event. And you've processed that energy to come up with a convincing narrative. I guess the next step would be to see if you're correct. How would we go about doing that?"

Turning the pipe tool in his fingers, he could just make out the worn engraved *B*. "Some answers we'll need to find the old-fashioned way—through research. As the girl was looking over the inscription, I did see this jeweler's mark. There's not much of it left, but with any luck, we might be able to figure out where the pipe tool was made. In New Orleans, family businesses don't disappear. They just get folded into whatever comes after them like the layers of old peeling paint on the walls."

"We should also go back to the antique gun shop. Remember he said the pipe tool came in with a collection of Civil War artifacts? Maybe he can put us in contact with the collector who sold him the stuff."

Myles wasn't crazy about returning to the gun shop and all its negative energy, but he didn't see much choice. Coming up with a story, real or make-believe, was one thing. Proving it would be closer to the areas of archeological research he'd hoped to leave to others.

---

a s a college student, Myles had studied the French Quarter, specifically Bourbon Street, every chance he got. Often, his explorations resulted in sitting in class the next day with a hangover. The research gave him a good grounding in which establishments to apply to after graduation. Though an archeology major, the only rocks he dug through these days were the ice cubes he used in making colorful concoctions for drunk tourists. Fellow service workers knew him in the Quarter. He thought he knew every business, from the historic, family-owned restaurants to the fly-by-night art galleries, even if some of them he seldom frequented.

The upscale jewelry store gave him the willies. Walking in with Kendell at his side made him thrust his hand into his pocket to protect his wallet. At least she wasn't his girlfriend, but the elegant lady who smiled and greeted them wouldn't know their relationship status. Men didn't often get dragged into stores displaying rings, necklaces, and other expensive items meant to enhance a woman's beauty without the expectation of purchasing at least a little something.

The saleswoman spread her bejeweled hands out on the crystal clear glass case filled with gold rings. "Can I help you find something? We have a lovely selection of black star sapphire earrings and necklaces."

At least she hadn't started pushing the engagement rings. He had to admit the woman had pegged Kendell perfectly.

In spite of their objective, Kendell couldn't help but stare at the gemstones. "They're beautiful."

"We have them in everything, from moderately priced earrings to elegant wedding bands. A wonderful aspect of star sapphires is they can be as easily worn by a man as a woman."

He feared that in another couple of minutes, the saleswoman would have Kendell's mind filled with ideas of where their nonexistent romance might end up. He pulled out the drawing he'd made of the calligraphy *B*. "Have you ever had a piece come through your shop with this mark?"

The store clerk managed to not look disappointed, but he suspected she'd just dropped her opinion of them from potential buyer to below casual browser. "Let me get Philip. He's our master jeweler."

She disappeared for a moment into the back room. When she returned, she hardly gave them a second glance, preferring instead to greet a new prospect who had just walked in.

A man with grizzled gray hair, glasses, and a leather

apron emerged a minute later with the piece of paper. "I don't see the Boudreaux jeweler's mark often. Your rendering looks like an older version, but I'd know the enlarged lower loop anywhere. I don't typically work on his pieces, out of professional courtesy, but if you've got a piece that needs something minor, I can have a look."

Myles tried to keep calm. "Are you saying they're still in business?"

"That would be overstating it. Henri only putters around the shop these days as a means of staying busy. He's kind of a curmudgeon, but not many of us know more about working precious metals than he does. I'll give you his address. If he proves too difficult to deal with or even locate, feel free to bring the piece to me, and I'll see what I can do. Work from Boudreaux's was always very high quality. Whatever you've got, I'll wager it's worth holding onto."

~

THEY WALKED past the arched carriage entrance of the creole townhouse three times before Myles realized there was something else beyond the gaudy paintings that hung on the alleyway's brick walls. He hadn't even known that the small jewelry shop tucked into the nook of the courtyard on Chartres existed. Walking through an artist's domain often meant interacting with the person, especially when what passed for a gallery wasn't even as wide as a driveway. Getting from the street to the back courtyard meant at least offering a brief word of encouragement to the hippie-looking woman behind the sunflower-yellow counter.

They passed through the long entrance that led to the intimate oasis bathed in early afternoon light. From the faded sign for Boudreaux's Fine Jewelry and the weathered wood, rippled-glass door, and dust that caked the front windows, the small shop looked to have been in business for generations. Though based on the appearance of the elderly gentleman who lounged half-asleep behind the workbench, the establishment might not survive to see another heir.

The sole proprietor roused himself as the antique bell that hung next to the door announced Myles and Kendell's entrance. Myles took only a passing glance at the displays filled with antique and custom-made rings and necklaces. Everything looked well crafted and expensive. *The man must know his stuff.* "I'm hoping you can help us. We ran across this pipe tool. From the mark near the inscription, we thought it might have come from this shop."

For a man probably in his seventies, the jeweler had a lot of dexterity. He used his fingers like finely tuned instruments of precision as he turned the pipe tool under the large magnifying lens. "You're correct. That mark does refer to this shop. That version of our family's insignia is very old. It dates back when we owned this whole building. Now all that's left is this little workshop. From the workmanship and fine detail of the engraving, I'd guess this piece to be from the 1850s. My forefather would have had to be in his early thirties to have the skills but also retain the eyesight needed to work with this level of precision."

Kendell seemed far more interested in what the jeweler

was inspecting than the expensive necklaces that sparkled all around her. "Can you make out the writing? Myles says he can read it, but I'm not convinced."

The artist-craftsman dabbed a cotton swab into a small jar and wiped the liquid across the old gold. "To My Father. Love, Serephine. Humph."

Myles didn't remember that last word from his dream. "What did we miss?"

The man looked up over the half lenses of his glasses. "I've done thousands of inscriptions and seen a lot more from my predecessors. This one is cold, formal. They used a stiff address as if enforcing the subtle message of personal separation more than family attachment. But then, I have a lot of time on my hands. Sometimes I read more into an inscription than is intended. There's also a family crest next to the engraving. I believe it refers to Baron Malveaux. He was the city's primary banker before the War Between the States—though the other items I've seen with that calligraphy *M* were much larger and more expensive. It you can leave the tool with me, I might have more information for you in a day or two."

Myles had a momentarily irrational hesitation about leaving the item with the jeweler. "Do you really need to keep the piece?"

The old man's dry chuckle seemed as at home in the small shop as the ancient metalworking tools. "Are you afraid I'll steal it or die on you?"

Kendell took Myles's hand. "It's a gift for my father. We just wanted a little backstory to go with the antique."

Mr. Boudreaux quickly sketched the family crest, an *M*

written in elegant calligraphy with skulls at the corners. Myles admired the ability of the old hands to so fluidly render the image. "Leave me your address, and I'll send over what I find."

Myles felt a twinge of anxiety as Kendell scrawled her information on a scrap of paper.

~

KENDELL UNDERSTOOD Myles's concerns about returning to the gun shop. After all, an item had tried to impale his foot. But to her, the place had a familiarity she found difficult to identify. They found the place in a flurry of activity and only received a passing "hello" as the clerk unscrewed a wooden crate behind the counter. In the back room, another box already had its lid removed. A man in jeans and dress shirt was gingerly removing the packing straw. He took out a long rifle with an elegantly carved silver stock.

Kendell inspected a dagger that had been left on the counter. "This must be the Napoleonic delivery."

Every sword, gun, and article of clothing looked too nice to have been used in battle.

The man in the back room looked up in surprise at having customers. "I'm afraid we get pretty consumed with curiosity when we get a new delivery. It's kind of like Christmas morning for us. What can I do for you?"

Kendell kept the gold cylinder in the pocket of her jacket. "We were in last week. We purchased a small pipe tool. We were hoping you might have some information about who sold you the piece."

The shop owner smiled like a fisherman who'd just gotten a bite on the line. "That's the way this passion starts. Antiques are as much about the story as the object. People always want to know were something came from. For the bigger items, like this collection we're unpacking, we get all we can from the seller. Partly, that's to ensure the items are real and not reproductions, but also, the knowledge helps us answer customers' questions."

Myles kept his hands in his pockets. "We were told the pipe tool came in with a Civil War collection."

"We get people walking in all the time with boxes of junk. Seems like every time a house changes hands, the new owner thinks they have discovered some archeological relic hiding in the attic that no one had ever noticed before. Most have no clue what they've got but are certain it's all worth a fortune. Sometimes junk really is just junk."

The clerk in the back turned away from the crate he was working on. "They're talking about those cardboard boxes that came in early this month. You remember? I think the stuff came from an architect's office in the Garden District."

The owner turned to the back room. "Right. I do remember." He shuffled through some papers in a beat-up metal desk. "Here it is—Laurette and Associates. I'm afraid I don't have much more than the name and address. I guess it'll be up to you to discover the piece's provenance. Just be careful. Collecting antiques can become addictive. Once you have one item, others seem to find you like you're holding a magnet to history."

Kendell looked around the shop. "Could you point out the other things that came in with the pipe tool?"

The owner nodded toward an old armoire. "There wasn't much worth displaying. My guess would be one of the founding members of the architectural firm might have fought for the South. Confederate memorabilia often ended up stashed away in closets or attics. I'll give you the address, but don't get your hopes up. By the time stuff like this surfaces, anyone who might remember the history is usually long gone."

The Confederate uniform was so moth-eaten that only the *a* of the officer's name was still identifiable. She searched along the dress sword for any distinguishing marks. From the overall condition of the collection, she suspected the storeowner was correct. The items hadn't been discarded, but clearly, no member of the family wanted to be reminded of their ancestor's ignoble past.

∾

MYLES IMAGINED that riding down Saint Charles Avenue in the vintage streetcar would instill New Orleans history into anyone with even a passing ability to detect human energy. Though countless people routinely used that form of public transportation for work, an even greater number used it for heading to the Quarter for fun or going home after an exhausting adventure.

He only ventured into the Garden District when visitors were in town. People liked to see the huge old mansions. Walking along the streets and reading the plaques that recounted meaningless history designed to increase the value of the high-maintenance structures was only fun the first time. Usually, he felt like some dumb tourist gawking through the windows at old people who'd rather be left alone.

Kendell compared the note to the address carved above the gate. "This is it."

"I thought the guy at the antique store said it was a place of business. This mansion looks like something that should be torn down." The home's problem wasn't unique. Every house that took up a quarter of a city block was either perfectly maintained, restored, or in complete shambles. Taking a mansion down to the studs and rebuilding it to period-correct glory was often more expensive than starting from scratch. The one they'd stopped at would make one badass haunted house, though.

"I see a car. Maybe there's someone we could talk to."

Yeah. Dracula. But Myles kept his sarcasm to himself. Vines held tight to the wrought-iron gate. The squealing racket the rusty hinges made as he leaned against the worn ornate metal should have been notification enough that the house had visitors. But no one rushed out to greet them or shoo them away. "You know, just once I'd like someone to tell us to go to some nice restaurant or modern friendly-looking home to find an answer."

"You're the archeologist." She pounded on the most structurally sound plank of the front door. The etched glass window that distorted the view of the interior rattled ominously.

Myles heard the footsteps from upstairs. The longer it took for the person to get to the front door, the worse he felt about intruding. *No wonder people who lived in these places had servants. Just greeting guests would have been a task.*

A woman with long blond hair, wearing dusty jeans and a Maroon 5 T-shirt, yanked open the warped door. "Unless you've got a bulldozer to help clean this mess up, I'm probably not interested in anything you're selling."

Kendell pulled out the pipe tool. "Actually, we're looking for a little information on something that may have come out of your cleaning efforts. We recently bought this in the Quarter, and the shop owner referred us to you."

The woman smudged her forehead as she wiped the hair away from her face. "I don't know what I could tell you. I found it stuffed into a wall of the attic. I'm just trying to declutter so I can figure out what to do with this dump."

The smell of rodent droppings and rotting wood wafted out toward Myles. "Do you know anything about the previous owners?"

"Not much. They were my grandparents. Please, come in if you can stand the smell. I'm afraid it only gets worse the deeper you go into this architectural ruin."

The floor creaked so loudly that Myles wondered if they might have been safer talking out on the porch. The den off the front foyer must have been something before the squares of rippled glass broke out of the windows. Vines crept up the walls from the openings. Wallpaper of red and gold curled down from the fifteen-foot-tall ceiling. The remains of drapes hung from pitted iron rods. He wouldn't have trusted his luck to the furniture, but since their hostess took a seat, he thought it'd be rude not to do likewise. It took a little adjusting to keep the couch spring from jabbing through his jeans.

Kendell chose to lean against the fireplace mantel. "I'm Kendell, and this is Myles. Thanks for taking the time to talk to us."

"Anything to get out of those upstairs closets. I'm Samantha Laurette. There was a time when the name Laurette meant something down here in New Orleans. I'm afraid now it just means *sucker who inherited a dump.*"

"How long did your grandparents live here?" Kendell asked.

"The house has been in my family for generations."

"But you didn't grow up here?"

Samantha looked around the weathered room. "I never lived here. And I'm not about to move in now. My father escaped to Atlanta as a college student and never looked back. He recently died of cancer, so I ended up having to deal with this nightmare. You can't imagine what the city of New Orleans considers a historic residence or what they will and won't let you do to it."

"You must have visited your grandparents when you were a kid, though," Kendell said. "I'll bet this place was really something in its day."

"I only remember it as looking dated even when it wasn't falling down. I think the last time they had it remodeled was in the 1970s. The kitchen's all done in avocado and brown. Even back then, it wasn't really an appetizing place for a meal if you know what I mean."

Myles took the pipe tool from Kendell. "There's a family insignia on here. Have you ever heard the name Malveaux?"

For just the briefest of moments, he thought the woman squinted at him, but it could have just been a trick of the light. "Can't say that I have. I've only just started digging through the boxes. The Civil War memorabilia looked like it might be valuable, so I tested the waters and went to the antique dealers with it. The more room I can make in the attic, the more space I'll have for organizing. Most of the cardboard boxes up there are so water damaged and chewed on by rodents that they're not salvageable. Somewhere in this maze of family history is a genealogical chart my grandfather was working on. Though with the overall condition of everything I've found so far, I'm not optimistic. I'm sorry I can't help you, but I really need to get back to work."

~

SITTING with Kendell in the outdoor beer garden on Magazine Street, Myles turned the small golden tube in his hand. He still couldn't identify what had made him ill at ease with the jeweler. The old man wouldn't have anything to gain from taking the pipe tool. Why was he being so paranoid about something so meaningless? And why had mentioning the name Malveaux resulted in Miss Laurette showing them the door?

Kendell put down her lager. "You're getting a little obsessed with that thing."

"I just had a creepy feeling of something bad happening if we left it with the jeweler."

"He seemed pretty harmless to me," she said.

It wasn't the man himself. That much Myles knew. "I'm not that adept at reading energy yet. I'm still learning. But there's something else about this piece beyond the story I told you. I can't identify what I'm experiencing. It's like I'm watching a horror-mystery movie and knowing the main character is about to do something stupid."

"Are you sure you're not just projecting our visit to the Laurette house onto your memories? It was just a run-down building. I'm surprised the place has stood as long as it has without proper maintenance. Poor Samantha. I don't know what I'd do if I was in her shoes. How would you even begin to sift through that much family history?"

"Typically, people ask for help." Myles remembered a lecture about historic items being passed down for generations until only one person remained. Most of the time, that individual had no interest in being the family's repository of junk. The savvy historian or shady antique dealer was always on the lookout for such opportunities. Samantha Laurette was too attractive and outgoing to not have friends who would drop everything to come help clean out a mansion in the Garden District. For most people, the adventure would prove enticement enough. So what was she doing in that old place all alone?

"At least we're a little closer to knowing who Serephine was than we were this morning. We know her last name was Malveaux. We know something of her father. I'm not sure the visit to the Laurette mansion told us anything, but there must be some connection between the two families. I wonder if Samantha ran across any old family diaries during her cleaning. Maybe we should try the museum achieves for any old news articles. You'd think the death of a famous banker's daughter would make it into the papers. Maybe not the front page, but it must have been mentioned somewhere."

Between running around town and the energy that he could still feel from the tool, all Myles wanted was some sleep. "There's still no proof I didn't imagine the whole story. Even the marks on the tool I could have seen and not realized until I was semiconscious. We don't know anything. All this running around is giving me a headache."

Myles could feel Kendell's eyes on him as he toyed with the cylinder and drank his dark porter. From the moment the jeweler had mentioned leaving the item in his shop, Myles hadn't been able to take his mind from the object.

A fear emanated from it, but it wasn't the emotion of the young child. He didn't remember feeling that apprehension in the morning. His anxiety had only started when they left the small workshop. The feeling grew more intense once they'd entered the Laurette house. He should have held the tool while they'd talked to Miss Laurette. She knew something, and he suspected the tool had responded to her. But with it resting in Kendell's hand, there had been no way of knowing.

Kendell dropped her spoon into her gumbo with such force some of it splashed out of the bowl. "Give that to me. It's affecting you somehow. I'll keep it safe tonight. We can pick this investigation up in the morning. You need to get some rest."

~

REST WOULD HAVE BEEN NICE, but being a bartender in the Quarter meant working late hours.

Myles flipped a bottle of vodka back onto the rack behind him. "Hey, Charlie, have you ever heard the names Malveaux or Laurette?"

His diving buddy and fellow bartender had a way with people. Myles never knew what tidbits of New Orleans history might be locked in his friend's ambitious head. "Never heard of Malveaux. Do you have any context?"

"From what I've gathered the baron Malveaux was a banker around the early 1800s. And the name Laurette refers to an architect, but I don't have a date on that one."

Charlie spun the bottle of tequila as he thought. "Well, if the Malveaux family was around before the Civil War, that might be your answer. A lot of family lines ended when they sent their boys to battle. Laurette, though—that one I do recognize. For generations, they designed mansions in the Garden District. I didn't think they were still around."

So far, Charlie wasn't awfully helpful, but anything beat having to talk to drunk tourists. "I was at what was left of the Laurette mansion today. The business must have closed up a long time ago. From the woman I talked to, I got the impression the family name might also be down to its last representative."

"That's a shame." Charlie grabbed a couple of plastic drink dispensers and headed toward the shot girl, who was waving her empty rack at him.

A group of drunk college boys fell into the side entrance next to Myles's end of the bar. One had the impudence to slam his Pat O'Brian glass on the bar. "Another hurricane!"

Some nights, it took all of Myles's tact not to do something that would get him fired. Instead of correcting the obnoxious idiot as to which bar he was in, Myles mixed up a drink strong enough to land the guy in the party juice of Bourbon Street's gutters.

Charlie nudged Myles's arm as he returned the bottles of colorful alcoholic drinks. "What's with the interest in New Orleans family lineages?"

"Just another flight of imagination."

Charlie leaned in conspiratorially to be heard over the latest '80s cover band on stage. "If you're onto something interesting, count me in. That World War II discovery got me laid for months."

"What about Vanessa?"

"Yep. That adventure got me in her panties too."

"I meant, aren't you two dating?" Myles had to yell to be heard over the mangled rendition of "Dance with Me."

Charlie held up two bottles of Abita Amber. "This is New Orleans!"

Not surprisingly, everyone at the bar yelled in agreement.

5

_K_endell changed into her oversized nightshirt and climbed under her billowy comforter. She wasn't tired, but she often did some of her best thinking cuddled up under the covers prior to falling asleep. Cheesecake took her protective position at Kendell's feet, facing the bedroom door.

The time with Myles had proven eventful. He'd given her a reason to get out of her apartment and into a new adventure. Not that finding guys to take her out had been a problem. Working at the coffee shop and playing at the Scratchy Dog afforded her plenty of interactions with people. But not having to fend off a man's advances meant she'd had the luxury of focusing on others rather than constantly playing defense. Myles was one of those rare nice guys who might or might not be interested in a sexual relationship. If he was just trying to fuck her, he was on the wrong track. Agreeing to explore the paranormal with her, like kids playing make believe, wasn't the quickest way into her panties. "Do you think he finds me attractive?"

From the way Cheesecake sighed and put her head down on her paws, Kendell knew the dog pitied and distrusted any guy who didn't see the wonders of her mistress.

"His lack of interest in having sex with me isn't a bad thing. We might even become friends, real friends, not like the other guys you've met."

The dog turned her big brown eyes to Kendell and rolled onto her back. It was a clear sign she either wanted a belly rub or wished to get some sleep. After eleven years, Kendell had learned the difference, but reading Cheesecake was often a matter of looking for subtleties. She was a complex being. Anyone who didn't get that wasn't someone Kendell wished to know.

"You could try to be a little nicer to him. It's not like he wanted to pick you up." Kendell reached down to rub Cheesecake's chest even though sleep was what she was after.

The dog rolled to her side to grasp Kendell's hand in her paws.

"Okay, my good girl. I'll let you get some rest."

Getting to know Myles purely for the enjoyment and adventure was good enough for the moment. She didn't need to be speculating on where he might want to take the relationship. She'd be on guard as always, and if she did slip, Cheesecake would be there to let her know. Kendell pulled the thick comforter up to her chin and gave her dog a gentle pat with her foot from under the covers before falling asleep.

It never took long for her to drift off on her luxurious bed. Her dream of living in New Orleans during the 1800s, however, was rudely interrupted by Cheesecake launching off the bed. The dog never was a deep sleeper, and the apartment on Decatur provided more than the occasional random street noise that would set her off to investigate.

But Cheesecake's barks weren't the usual announcement of a group of loud drunks below her apartment. Kendell bolted out of bed as she recognized the threatening howl that said someone was in their domain. As she rushed out of the small bedroom and into the moonlit living room, she saw her normally reserved dog fly into an all-out attack against what had originally looked like nothing more than a shadow. The inner wolf, once provoked, would never back down once she felt threatened. But this was the first time Kendell knew they really were in danger.

Cheesecake had the hooded intruder by the sleeve of his dark leather coat and was wildly shaking her head like a dog possessed. The burglar held something in his hand, but he wasn't using it as a weapon.

"Leave my dog alone, and get out of my apartment!" Even though Cheesecake was dominating the fight, Kendell couldn't stand the idea of her dog in danger. She looked around for something to throw at the burglar. But before she could grab the nearby glass vase, the man let out a yell of pain and dropped whatever he had in his hand.

Even in the moonlight, Kendell could make out the blood that oozed from the bite mark on his wrist. Having freed the item in danger of being stolen, the dog let go of the man's arm and lunged for the object. Kendell had only the briefest glimpse of the gleaming pipe tool as her dog took it into her mouth and swallowed it.

"Crazy dog, what do you think you're doing?"

Apparently, the burglar must have had a similar thought as he snatched Cheesecake off the floor and bolted for the open window to the balcony.

This can't be happening. It has to be a bad dream. "What are you doing? Put my dog down, asshole!" Kendell chased after them as Cheesecake wriggled, growled, and attempted to bite her abductor. In their eleven years together, she'd never heard her dog fight with such animal aggression. But size was still against her.

Kendell chased after the pair, screaming out Cheesecake's name as they disappeared over the balcony railing and down the metal fire escape. In her panic she tripped over the window ledge and hit her head on the chaise lounge she used as her quiet reading place. By the time she got off the porch floor, the thief had made his escape with her dog.

MYLES WASN'T the deepest of sleepers, but coming to always proved disorienting. When his cell phone woke him, he struggled to find the off button to what he assumed was the alarm. Instead of the phone going quiet so he could fall back asleep, however, Kendell's panicked voice brought him to full-alert status. "Someone's stolen Cheesecake! Oh God, Myles, get over here. I don't know what to do. Please help me!"

He'd never gotten out of bed, dressed, and crossed a handful of blocks so fast in his life. The only thought that kept running around in his mind was *Why would anyone steal a pet?* Some things were strictly off-limits. He could envision no reason for the abduction. *Poor Kendell.*

Her door flew open as he bounded up the stairs to her apartment. Her hands were shaking and tears streamed down her face as she gasped out the words, "They dognapped her. They stole my sweet girl."

He took her into his arms, unsure of what else to do. "Don't worry. We're going to get her back."

As she recounted her story, she had to take a sobbing breath between each word. His emotions made it hard to focus. The natural instinct to rush outside and start hunting for the dog struggled with the intellectual need to hear what had happened, and that, unfortunately, was frustrated by Kendell's inability to quickly tell her story.

He looked out the window that had been jimmied open to the balcony. He didn't want to let go of Kendell while she was still in shock, but finding the dog took priority.

She nodded toward the open window as he let her go. "He ran out that way."

Like most of the streets in that area of the Quarter, life never stopped, even on a Wednesday in winter at one in the morning. Peering over the wrought-iron railing, Myles saw the usual array of gutter punks. "Hey, did any of you see a guy jump down from the fire escape with a dog?"

A skinny dude holding a bottle of Jack Daniels in one hand and a slice of pizza in the other pointed the triangle of cheese and pepperoni down Decatur. "That thing was a dog? I thought for sure it was some kind of demon. Sure didn't sound like a dog. I've never heard anything like it. That dude holding it had some balls, I'll tell ya."

Myles wasn't really interested in the drunk youth's opinions. "Did he get in a car? Which way did they go? That asshole stole my friend's pet."

"Dude. That's not cool. I'd have punched that guy if I'd known and wasn't so afraid of that demon."

A young woman with ratty-looking blond dreadlocks stepped in for her drunk companion. "He jumped in a truck loaded with portable generators and speakers. He was headed toward Jackson Square."

"Those were some sweet woofers." From the way the drunk gutter punk shook his head, Myles suspected that if the truck been left on Decatur much longer, it might have been missing a couple of items off the back.

He grabbed Kendell's arm to stop her from pacing. "Go put some clothes on. I think I know where he was headed. We're going after Cheesecake."

Kendell's eyes were larger than those of any woman he'd known as she looked hopefully at him. "Thank you."

"Don't thank me until we get her back. I'm not leaving your side until we do."

6

*K*endell's bright-yellow Vespa scooter had the advantage of being small enough to dodge the potholes that scarred every street in New Orleans. But speed and safety weren't its strong points. Myles twisted the accelerator grip so hard he thought he must be stretching the cable. Not that the increased pressure made the damn thing move any faster. Snuggled up to his back, Kendell had at least stopped sobbing. He could feel her desperation as she gripped him around the waist. They were doing something, and that at least meant she wasn't sitting around her apartment in a state of panic.

"Where are we going?"

He reached down to rub her arm as she hugged him tight. "Float World. The only reason someone would need a bunch of generators and speakers would be for a Mardi Gras parade. Cheesecake will be all right. Why on Earth would anyone want to steal your dog, anyway?"

"I don't know. They were fighting over that damn pipe tool, but it's not like that was worth anything. I'd have let him have it instead of losing my girl."

Myles continued rubbing her arm as he swung the scooter toward the row of warehouses that lined the wharf along the Mississippi River. He'd have given up the object too. The question kept nagging him of why someone would want it so badly as to break the law. However, it wasn't like the cops were going to do much about an abducted dog or a stolen pipe tool, at least not at one in the morning.

Kendell pulled tighter against his stomach. "You really think he was headed to the warehouses?"

"If he wanted to wait until Cheesecake pooped out the pipe tool, that area would be isolated enough that no one would hear the barking."

It wouldn't help her state of mind to tell her what he really thought. If the thief just wanted the pipe tool, killing the dog—much as Myles hated to admit it—would have been the simplest of solutions. The fact that he hadn't harmed Cheesecake when she bit him gave Myles hope. The person either had a conscience or needed the dog alive. Either way, Myles would have time to rescue the dog, and ultimately, that was the most important thing.

He parked the scooter next to a pickup truck that had been backed up to a loading dock. He felt the commercial vehicle's exhaust pipe. It was still hot. The gaudily painted warehouse had a creepy-carnival haunted-house feel to it during the day. At night, the dark buildings made his skin crawl.

Kendell grabbed his arm. "I know you said not to tell you

until we find Cheesecake, but thank you for doing this. It means a lot to me."

"In spite of what my family thinks, I didn't go into archeology to be the next Indiana Jones. But I suppose if the opportunity for adventure and the need to save a damsel in distress presents itself, I'd be a fool not to take the challenge. Even if the damsel happens to be a dog."

"You don't think they'd hurt her, do you?" He could tell from her quivering voice it wasn't a prospect she wanted to consider, but walking into a potentially dangerous situation forced the question.

"Whoever did this hasn't hurt her yet, so I think she'll be okay. Just the same, the sooner we find her and get the hell out of here, the better."

They crept around the corner to the gaping entrance. As they entered the darkened warehouse, large, sculpted clown heads faced them from either side. "And I thought this place was creepy enough from outside." *Poor Cheesecake. Hold on, girl. We're coming.*

A trail of fresh blood directed them down the center of the cement floor between the towering floats.

"You don't think that's Cheesecake's blood, do you?" Kendell's quivering voice indicated her failure to calm her sense of panic.

"My money would be on Cheesecake being the aggressor. There was blood on your balcony too. I don't think that guy knew what he was getting into when he took her. We'll keep to the shadows." He only hoped he sounded believable. Having Kendell in a state of distress wasn't going to help keep them undetected.

The thought of Cheesecake getting another bite of the thief gave him only a passing sense of smug satisfaction. Hopefully, he was right, and they were keeping her alive for some reason he couldn't figure out. *I wish we'd never laid eyes on that damn pipe tool.*

As they moved deeper into the cavernous warehouse, the light from the door cast their shadows like giant, skinny, ghostly specters. "We need to get closer to the floats so they don't see us." But walking under the figureheads and over the tow bars used by the tractors was slow going.

She held tight to his hand as if she were afraid she'd lose him. "How are we going to see anything in here?"

The penlight he pulled from his pocket didn't inspire confidence. It did, however, illuminate a jester's head six feet tall. She gripped his hand hard. At least she didn't scream at the colorful apparition.

He crouched between two floats that smelled of fresh paint. "Let your eyes adjust for a moment. If they're in here, there will be a light on somewhere. They'll probably be in one of the back offices."

One of the side benefits to working nights was that given enough time, his eyesight could adjust to almost any lighting conditions. It wasn't the sight of the creepy clowns and jesters that caught his attention but the sound of a wolf snarling that echoed around the cavernous building.

Standing close behind him, Kendell grabbed his hand. "I've never heard Cheesecake growl like that before."

Though her assessment made the most logical sense, he had trouble envisioning the elderly overweight lapdog reverting to her ancestral roots. "That does not sound like your dog—more like some wild animal."

Her short hair teased his cheek as she shook her head. "You might be surprised. Lhasa apsos are only one layer of domestication from the Tibetan mountain wolf. That's one of the things I love about her. She hasn't had all that natural instinct bred out of her."

Two beams of light hit the sculpted glittery faces that adorned the floats on either side of the central passage. Cheesecake-the-wolf let out another warning snarl from halfway down the warehouse, attracting whoever was wielding the flashlights.

Myles grabbed Kendell's wrist. "Let's hide in the float. We can see what's going on better, and we'll have the advantage of being above whoever might be coming. Just stay quiet. Sounds carry in here."

They snuck around to the back of the long trailer decorated to look as if the court jesters had taken over the castle. The wood steps creaked as they made their ascent, but Cheesecake's growls would have commanded the attention of anyone on the prowl.

The voices of two men carried clearly to the second-floor stage of the float.

"Damn dog. Why did you let it escape? We'll be looking for dog shit for days if we don't find it soon."

"You're not the one who got bit, so stop complaining. That thing may look like a fat, lazy animal, but it's got the heart of a killer. When I get my hands on that beast—"

"You're not going to do anything. Remember the

contract. No living thing is to suffer harm while in possession of the pipe tool."

"Yeah, well, they didn't say anything about a person or animal *not* in possession of a Malveaux object."

"Just shut up and keep looking. Maybe we should split up."

"Not on your life. I don't know how that little girl managed to keep a vicious animal in that apartment, but I've learned my lesson. We stick together."

Kendell gripped Myles's arm so hard he started losing feeling in his hand. "She's okay. I'm going to go get her. Stay here. If they catch me, you'll be my way out."

"Are you crazy? I'm pretty sure those assholes have guns. Sounds to me like Cheesecake has this covered."

She turned to him like he was the one who sounded insane. "She doesn't know they won't hurt her. Neither do we. I can sneak down there and find her before they do. She always knows when I'm around. She'll find me."

Myles grabbed her arm. "Leave me your phone in case I need to call for help."

She gave him the familiar look he received from most of his ex-girlfriends. "Where's yours?" But instead of waiting for the typical lame answer that it never fit in his jeans, she just shook her head and handed him her phone.

Even with his eyesight adjusted to the warehouse, Kendell in her black floor-length jacket appeared like a shadow darting from dark passageway to towering float. His heart beat faster as he searched for some sign of her. *Great. Now I've lost both Kendell and her dog.*

He stopped breathing at Cheesecake's next set of barks.

They weren't the howls of anger but the welcoming yelps of seeing Kendell. *Damn it, dog. Now you've put her in danger.* Cheesecake's change of mood also attracted the two men with flashlights.

Myles had Kendell's phone out and was texting Polly Urethane, her most recent contact, before the beams of light converged between the floats so far away.

The conversation carried crisp and clear to his perch. "Okay, girl. Come on out from under that float. I see you, and I've got a gun. Bring your dog."

His heart sank as he watched Kendell emerge into the beams of light holding Cheesecake in her arms. "You can have the damn pipe tool. I don't even want it. Cheesecake will listen to me. I can keep her calm. She's not going to do her business if she's feeling threatened. All I'm asking is once you have your fucking tool back, let us go. I'm no threat to you. It's not worth anything, and so far, no one's been hurt."

The men apparently had the same thought as one of them grabbed two Mardi Gras masks off the float. From his elevated position, Myles could see the two men whispering to each other while Kendell and Cheesecake stood in the bright beams of their flashlights. She wouldn't have been able to see their faces.

"Are you alone?"

Of course not, you moron. A young woman's just going to go chasing after the guy who stole her dog in the middle of the night all on her own? How stupid are you? Myles prayed they were exactly that stupid.

He could hear from Kendell's tone that she too

63

considered the question to be one of the dumber ones she'd heard, but she turned that judgmental attitude to her advantage. "Of course I'm alone. Who do you think would be up at this hour to drop everything and come looking with me?"

"The police maybe?"

Even the second thug thought that unlikely. "Think. If she'd called the police, she'd be the last person in this warehouse. We'd have been safe for days instead of hours if the authorities were in charge. She's just some foolish girl who loves her dog. Her help might not be a bad idea."

Thug number one tried to redeem himself as he addressed Kendell. "Don't try anything stupid. We gave your hellhound a laxative, so hopefully, we can part company before morning."

From Cheesecake's continued barking and whining, Myles suspected she wasn't on board with the negotiations. Kendell sat down in the middle of the corridor that ran the length of the warehouse and started singing to her dog. Cheesecake's whimpering calmed down by the end of Kendell's a capella rendition of "Bridge over Troubled Water."

Between songs, Kendell walked Cheesecake up and down the warehouse to see if she was any closer to being free of the pipe tool. Myles had to admire her subtlety. Each time she sat back down, she'd moved a float or two closer to him. He still didn't have a plan, but he had support. Polly and her crew had managed to sneak in and were strategically positioned on the neighboring floats—though

Myles doubted any of them had anything to use against the thugs other than a killer riff.

As quietly as possible, he rummaged through the heavy vinyl bags filled with Mardi Gras throws, seeking something he could toss out to distract the thugs should the need arise. Most of what he found were plastic doubloons and the ever-present beads—the Krewe of Rex floats tended to specialize in lightweight baubles. *Why couldn't I have climbed onto a Zulu float? A nice case of coconuts would be perfect.* Unzipping the next sack, he nearly threw down the bag of plush animals in disgust.

Having gotten a good idea of what lay in the bags, Myles progressed halfway down the float to a stack of cardboard boxes. *Cups. Great. I can offer to get them all drinks. That should be helpful.* He closed his eyes tight to fight back the frustration. As if the corralling of his mental energy had summoned what he needed, he opened the next box. His heart beat with increased adrenaline as he picked up the white plastic Frisbee embossed with the Rex emblem. *This is more like it.* Keeping low to avoid any possibility of being seen in the darkness, he hauled the box to the front of the float and set it next to the sacks of beads still tightly packed in their smaller plastic bags.

The thugs might always honor the agreement, though that wasn't a hope he dared rely on. Kendell might not have seen their faces, but she'd heard their voices and knew where they worked. The strongest case in her favor was the one the thug himself had come up with. So long as the only crime was the theft of a meaningless piece of crap, the police probably wouldn't even care—especially if the dognapped animal had been returned.

The assailants kept a healthy distance from Cheesecake, who continued to growl at the men in her low-pitched vibrato anytime Kendell's singing diminished. But after an hour, which felt more like ten, the dog grew tired of keeping up the threats. No sooner did Kendell set her down after the latest serenade of "I've Got You Babe" than the dog headed straight toward Myles. She only made it halfway before taking up the familiar squat position. Two flashlight beams converged on Cheesecake's behind. Myles felt bad for the dog. No one, not even an animal, would want to be so closely observed as they took a dump.

He couldn't remember ever waiting so impatiently for a dog to take a shit.

Thug number one said to his compatriot, "Go pick it up."

"Fuck you. It's her dog. She can get it."

One of the light beams dropped to the man's feet. "I'm not risking her throwing voodoo-doggie doo-doo at me. We both know the stories of the Malveaux objects. Do you really want your obituary to read 'He died covered in dog shit'?"

"Fine, I'll do it. But she's got to move that animal first. I'm not getting my arm bit off picking up dog crap."

Myles waited until Kendell had backed as far as she dared from the two thugs. One still held his gun on her as she once again held Cheesecake in her arms. The other bent down to pick up the poo with an empty bead bag. The instant Myles hit Send on Kendell's phone, four bright beams of light from the floats around him hit the two abductors. But momentary blindness was only the first of the two men's problems.

Myles flung the Mardi Gras Frisbee as hard as he could toward the ground between him and the gunman. It ricocheted off the cement floor and caught the man in the wrist. The gun went flying under one of the floats without ever getting off a shot. The next flying disk, however, sailed clear over the other abductor's head. Myles knew he had to calm down. Even in college, his nerves tended to get the better of him, messing up his aim, when he played on the disc golf team.

From behind the bright flashlights, Polly and the Strippers started throwing tightly packed bags of beads. Some burst open on the floor like fireworks, releasing brightly colored plastic beads and strands. Others beaned the men directly on their heads. The man bent over Cheesecake's poop barely scooped it up before being pummeled so hard he risked succumbing to the death by dog poop his compatriot had worried about.

From the float closest to Myles, a colorful decorated shoe from the Krewe of Muses struck the thief Myles had disarmed, hitting him in the head. As the man leaned back in shock his feet slipped on the growing layer of loose beads that had broken loose from the flimsy strands.

Even during a parade, gently lobbed strings of beads didn't always hold together. And often the drunk people demanding to be thrown something had to cover their heads from the onslaught. But used as projectiles thrown in anger, the small plastic beads and medallions proved more effective than Myles would have suspected.

"Have you got all the shit yet? We need to get the hell out of here." The thug farthest from Myles was still having trouble getting off the cement floor due to the beads. So long as he didn't go for the gun that had been lost under the float, his flight instinct would hopefully win out over the impulse to counterattack.

"Don't yell at me. I've got this damn dog shit all over my hands."

"Leave the shit. Just grab the pipe tool." As the abductor finally made it to his feet another colorfully decorated high-heeled shoe struck him in the seat of this pants.

"Got it." The thug closest to Myles had suffered the worst of the two. Beads of yellow, green, and purple were embedded in the brown slop that covered his arms and hands. He crawled away from the constant bombardment of brightly colored mementoes of revelry until he found a bare section of cement floor. Then he got to his feet and ran after his compatriot. Both men continued to slip on the plastic beads that worked like ball bearings on the cement floor.

Polly Urethane and the Strippers—being hopped up on adrenaline from their success—screamed taunts after the men as they made a run for it. Cheesecake's barks of hatred as she was once again safely in Kendell's arms made it clear she favored the band's idea of pursuit.

Myles let loose an ear-piercing whistle. "Let's get out of here. There's no point in putting ourselves in more danger."

The question of why someone would want the pipe tool enough to try and steal it—or worse, kidnap a dog over it—still plagued Myles. But getting Kendell and Cheesecake home safely won out over pursuing the thugs for answers.

7

*S*afely outside the warehouse, Kendell gave huge hugs to each of her bandmates. "I can't believe you guys came out to help me without even considering the danger. You can't imagine what this means to me. Band members for life!"

The others raised their fists along with Kendell in reply. "Band members for life!"

Myles too experienced the giddy adrenaline rush, but there were still practical matters to consider. He pulled out Kendell's phone. "We should call the cops."

She reached for his arm. "And tell them what? Some guys stole a fifty-dollar pipe tool from us? They held guns on us while we were trespassing in the warehouse? Even what we think we know isn't going to help sway the authorities to our side. I've got Cheesecake back, and that's all that matters."

He knew she was probably right. The most likely

outcome of calling in the authorities was they'd all be thrown in jail for breaking and entering. Then all the dognapper would have to do was say the dog went crazy biting him, and poor Cheesecake would be in real trouble.

Minerva pulled out the keys to her van. "Well, if we're not going after those assholes, and we're not waiting around for the cops, I guess we'd better get out of here before they wise up and realize bullets are stronger than beads. Can we give you a ride home?"

Kendell snuggled to his side. "We'll be all right on the scooter."

Polly looked over at the small yellow Vespa. "You sure? The two of you plus Cheesecake is going to be a tight fit. Your dog still looks pretty agitated."

Though still growling and whining at everyone else, Cheesecake nuzzled Myles's arm before lifting her head to lick his face. Kendell smiled up at him. "We'll manage. I'll give you girls a call when we get home. It'd hardly do for me to leave my knight in shining armor after he came to my rescue."

The band waited until he'd gotten the scooter started before climbing into the old VW. Kendell was still holding Cheesecake in her arms as she squeezed onto the back of the small seat. The motorbike swung side to side as he gunned the engine to build up enough speed for stability. As he turned onto the main road, he heard Minerva's van start up.

The ride back to Kendell's apartment proved more harrowing than he had expected. Between the small tires that found every pothole and the dog in Kendell's arms who, though rescued, seemed to still harbor feelings of hostility, he was having one hell of a time keeping the Vespa upright. "Is she okay back there?"

With only one of Kendell's hands on his side, the prospect of losing her off the back wasn't helping with his driving. "Just get us home."

What do you think I'm doing—going for some demented joyride? Myles stifled his frustration. It'd been a long night, and he knew his emotions were on edge as the adrenaline slowly wore off.

Though it was only a mile or two from the warehouse to Kendell's apartment, by the time he parked the small Vespa, both his passengers were about to fall asleep. "You two will want to get some rest. I'll talk to you in the morning."

Kendell flung Cheesecake over her shoulder so she could grasp Myles's arm. "Please don't go. I'd feel better if you came upstairs. I know it's late, but I'd appreciate the company. Or you can just sleep on the couch if you're tired."

He mentally kicked himself for being so dense. Of course she wouldn't want to be alone after having her apartment burglarized and her dog stolen. "I'd be happy to stay." The dark, narrow stairway would have been frightening enough without the evening's events. He took the keys from her trembling hand. "Let me go up first and make sure everything's okay. I can't imagine they'd come back as they got what they wanted. All the same, I'd feel better if you waited out here in the light for a moment."

"Thank you."

It might have been the desire for a shameless display of gallantry, or maybe it was just the experience of coming to her rescue, but he almost hoped there was someone on the other side of the paint-chipped door. His heart beat faster as he swung it open. There was no one waiting to pounce on him. He turned on every light he encountered as he walked through the small apartment. The furniture was still in disarray, but as he worked his way to the still-open window, he straightened what he could of the crime scene. The last thing Kendell would want to see was a reminder of her terror. He leaned over the balcony. "It's safe."

She didn't put the dog down until she'd looked in every corner of the small apartment. He feared it'd be days before either she or her dog felt completely safe in their own home.

Cheesecake was calmer, having passed the pipe tool, but completely drained. She reminded him of someone who'd spent three days on a bender and was suffering the consequences. He scratched her ears as she lay on the couch next to him.

Kendell brought out a bottle of Chardonnay and a couple of glasses. "I need a drink. For once, I wished I kept hard alcohol in the apartment. Hope you don't mind white wine."

It wasn't his favorite. Wine in general seemed like something that should only be drunk during family get-togethers, but he'd take damn near anything that would put his heart back on an even rhythm. "I'll pour. You still look a little shaky."

Her laugh as she looked at her quivering hands betrayed her state of delayed shock. "Guess I'm not as much of a badass as I'd like to pretend."

He filled the drinking glasses, giving her twice what he'd normally serve a patron ordering wine. "Don't sell yourself short. You stood your ground against those thugs. Anyone would be scared shitless having a gun pointed at them. I was amazed at how you were able to sing so calmly to Cheesecake during the ordeal."

She took a good long drink before setting the glass down. "She was scared and angry. She's always known what I was feeling. If I'm mad, she'll stay close to me but give me my space. When a relationship has ended, she'll lie next to me and won't take her head off my leg. I guess maybe I understand her too. But whatever she was feeling, it wasn't just the normal emotions. There was something in how she growled, something primal. As I sang to her, I could feel that wild instinct subside. But as soon as I'd finish a song, I could tell that untamed reaction was returning. It was like she was possessed or something. I wouldn't say this to anyone but you. And then only because we're trying to figure out this weird ability you have to read past energy. It sounded like those abductors were talking about a curse or something. With the way Cheesecake acted all strange after she swallowed the thing, it makes me wonder."

Myles shook his head. "You think some witch put a curse on that silly little pipe tool? I could understand what the professor was trying to say in that weird class. Psychometry isn't science, but it's close enough that I can see how one day it could be. But curses, witches, voodoo—those all sound too much like stories that are used to sell walking tours."

The topic of conversation wasn't what he'd have chosen,

but anything to distract her from the night's adventure could only help.

As she talked and drank her wine, her hands stopped shaking. Maybe having him to argue with gave her a direction for all that pent-up energy. "Why is it so hard for you to see the next step? First we accept that human energy can be left behind in a physical object. Then we observe that people like you can experience that energy. So far, intense emotions, like fear, are easiest for you to read. The next step is so obvious. Someone—a witch or a voodoo priestess or whatever—figures out how to intentionally load up an object with human energy. You said it yourself. That pipe tool gave you a headache. What if that feeling is the result of some curse?"

Myles frowned at her and kept petting Cheesecake, who seemed to enjoy his attention. "I'm trying to learn basic math, and you're talking advanced calculus."

Getting riled up about a topic brought back the Kendell he knew. "Religions all over the world believe they can bless an object. How would that be any different than cursing one? It'd just depend on what kind of energy was being pumped into the thing."

He grabbed a pillow and stuck it under his head with Cheesecake cuddled against his side. "I'm going to let you develop your idea without my input for a little while if that's okay."

~

THE EARLY AFTERNOON light through the eight-foot-tall

windows of Kendell's apartment illuminated Myles's dreams with a dull red background. The subtle change managed to wake him from his dream of being a medieval knight doing battle on his trusty stead, which had an unusual underbite.

Sleeping in one position on the couch had left his muscles aching. He pulled off the crocheted afghan that had been draped over him and looked around the apartment. Only Cheesecake seemed to be home. Her tired eyes kept watch over him from the ottoman. "Is Kendell at work, girl?"

The dog didn't respond. He wasn't sure how she'd react to him getting up. Sleeping, he hadn't provided much of a threat, but his moving around her mistress's apartment might not be so well accepted.

"I'm just going to remind you that it was me who helped rescue you last night. I'm not taking all the credit, but I feel I've earned a level of trust from you."

He worked his way to his feet while the dog watched. *So far so good.* With most women, Myles would attempt a polite overture first thing in the morning. For a dog, that would translate to a pet or a treat. But after the night Cheesecake had endured, Myles chose to view her more as a woman feeling under the weather than a wary dog. Trying not to look like he was sneaking around the apartment, he did his best to keep the noise down as he began his day.

By the time Kendell walked through the door, Cheesecake had moved to the patch of sunlight near the large window, and Myles had finished his cup of coffee. She smiled at the domestic scene. "I didn't want to wake you. I hope you and Cheesecake got along okay. I worried that locking her in my room while I was away would set her off."

He looked over at the dog, who appeared too well fed and comfortable to have been the same demonic wolf of the night before. "She's tolerating my presence. I'm not usually all that social when I have a hangover, and she's kind of displaying that same level of engagement."

Kendell dropped her embroidered-canvas bag on the kitchen table. "I think our next step is obvious. We need to go back to Boudreaux's jewelry store and see what he knows about this Malveaux family. We still need to discover if the story you dreamt—or imagined or whatever you want to call it—was true."

"We could just drop the whole thing."

"Are you crazy?" Kendell asked. "I'd say we're making real progress. Plus, we may be the only two people who understand why this thing is dangerous."

"So what? Is it really our obligation to try and stop something that we're only imagining? As for my so-called skills, what use are they if I'm putting us in danger?"

Kendell sat on the overstuffed chair. "Aren't you even a little bit curious? I am. For the first time in my life, I feel like I'm onto something important. Let me ask you this: why didn't you want to leave the pipe tool with Mr. Boudreaux?"

Things would have been so much easier if he had. "It'll sound stupid."

"Try me. When are you ever going to learn? I'm on your side."

He had to admit she was the first person not to laugh at him for what others considered an overactive imagination.

She believed in him. "While we were in the jeweler's shop, it was like Serephine was holding my hand. I had this overwhelming emotion of being trusted to do the right thing."

"Like you were there to protect her?" Kendell asked.

"I told you it'd sound stupid. I can't protect a little girl who committed suicide before my great-great-grandparents were even born."

The trust in her eyes gave him the same feeling of being counted on to do the right thing. "No, but maybe you can protect someone else from getting hurt. Even though we don't have the tool anymore, let's just see what we're up against. That jeweler must have found something."

He couldn't tell if she had a lust for adventure or an overly developed desire to protect others. "Have you considered that he might not be innocent in last night's adventures? Whoever wanted that thing had to find out about it from someone, and they had to know where you lived. Other than the shop where we bought it, he's the only one who fits that description."

She bit her lip as she looked at Cheesecake basking in the sunlight. "He seemed like such a sweet old man. That antique store didn't have any reservations about giving us Samantha Laurette's address. I would guess if someone asked about us, they would have given out my information too."

"Doesn't that frighten you? After last night, I'd think you'd want to stay as far from anyone connected to that pipe tool as possible."

Her eyes sparked from the sunlight like the black star

sapphires they'd encountered just before descending into this roller coaster of an adventure. "Cheesecake taught me not to back down from a fight. If we do nothing, we're just sitting ducks. Those guys last night can't be sure I didn't see them, and we know they have some connection to Float World. I don't know what they're planning, but I doubt it ends with the stealing of a fifty-dollar antique. I have no intention of sitting around, playing the scared victim cowering in her apartment. We don't have to confront them, but I need more information before I'll feel at ease again."

he old jeweler smiled as Myles escorted Kendell back into the shop. Myles still considered it more than likely that the old man had been the source of their misery, but whether his betrayal had been intentional or just a matter of letting the information slip to the wrong person was still to be discovered.

"I'm glad you two came back." The old man disappeared for a moment into the back room. He returned with a file folder filled with receipts. "It took more digging than I expected. I ended up spending half the night going through family files, ledgers, and notebooks. Somehow, in the mountain of information, I lost the small slip of paper with your address on it."

Or someone stole it. In spite of Myles's misgivings, he really hoped Mr. Boudreaux was telling the truth. But even if he was being honest, someone close to the old man might need investigating.

"My great-great-great-grandfather was Pierre Lafitte Boudreaux. Apparently, somewhere in my family tree there's a little pirate blood." The wink from Mr. Boudreaux didn't help with Myles's anxiety. "He inherited this building from his father, who was the first jeweler in our family. The early 1800s in New Orleans was a pretty fabulous time to be alive if you were a white rich man with property. Slavery and cotton were booming. So Pierre's father did quite well. Unfortunately, by the 1840s, when Pierre inherited the business, the bottom had dropped out."

Myles wondered if this story was going to take all day. Being an archeology major had meant hours of rambling stories told by just such old men who had nothing better to do than bore the hell out of anyone who'd listen. He'd learned the hard way that interrupting only meant the story would have to be started over from the beginning.

"Being an artist working in precious metals and stones has never been cheap. Even back then, people wanted variety. By the time I took over, there was already a healthy inventory from my predecessors. But poor Pierre was still trying to build our family's reputation. His skills were quite impressive, as you've noticed. But he needed money, and a lot of it, to keep perfecting his craft and building the business. That's where the baron Archibald Baptiste Malveaux comes in."

Finally. The mention of the name Malveaux heightened Myles's attention.

Mr. Boudreaux talked as if he knew the baron personally, leaving Myles to wonder how much of the story was based on facts and how much made up to fill in the gaps. "The baron ran the major bank back then. Most of the building boom that followed the economic depression of the early 1840s was financed through his institution. But he wasn't just an acute businessman. With his eye for political talent, he managed to get a number of powerful people elected at both the city and state levels. Why he didn't pursue the national stage is a mystery, but in the days leading up to the War Between the States, I suppose he felt more comfortable keeping his influence close to home."

The night before had been a late one filled with emotional upheaval. Though Mr. Boudreaux had a pleasant enough storytelling style, Myles feared he would fall asleep on his feet while listening to him.

"Pierre was small potatoes in the baron's eyes. The business was much too small to warrant a loan, and my family has never been much for politics. Pierre and the baron wouldn't have crossed paths. So when the elegant, well-dressed man in his thirties came into the jewelry shop looking for a headpiece to his walking cane, Pierre saw him as a much-needed client and not much else. I fear that lack of reading people might be a family trait."

"What is a headpiece?" Kendell leaned forward on the glass display case, clearly more fascinated with the story than Myles.

Mr. Boudreaux pointed to a nicely carved wooden barrel by the front door filled with walking canes. "From the moment the baron commissioned Pierre, every walking cane that left this shop was topped with some kind of head or skull. For the baron, Pierre fashioned a highly detailed silver skull. According to the journals, and borne out by the financial statements, that skull head was the beginning of Pierre's reputation as jeweler to the rich and powerful. But no matter how successful Pierre got, he'd always push aside the other orders for a new commission from the Malveaux family. Unlike many of the upper class of the time, the baron wanted his children to know the value of money. So though he'd lavish gifts on his wife and spend freely on himself, little Serephine would have had to save her allowance to purchase that pipe tool and have it engraved."

"You got all that from those receipts?" Myles knew he was letting his irritation get the better of him.

Mr. Boudreaux produced the yellowed slip of paper. "He mentioned on the tag that he discounted the engraving 'for the precious child.' I've looked through a bunch of these sales slips. Discounting his product was not common practice for Pierre."

Kendell eyed the expensive rings in the glass cabinet under her arms. "She must have really loved her father."

"I only know what my forefather wrote and the newspaper clippings he saved. The Malveaux family dynamic wasn't splashed all over the news like our modern-day celebrities. I suppose my predecessor thought it useful to gather what information he could on his most valued customer. With the baron's connections, no reporter would have the nerve to write something controversial, so Pierre jotted down his personal observations to go along with the articles. All I know is Serephine killed herself in her father's office at home within a year of giving him the pipe tool. Apparently, the banker took the death of his daughter hard. Pierre didn't receive any more commissions from the family. I suppose the pipe tool carried too many bad memories. Of course, the War Between the States dominated most of the news not long after the girl's death, so it's no surprise that I couldn't find anything else regarding the Malveaux family. There was a son, but he must have died in the war. I couldn't find any information on him."

"I don't mean to sound forward, but did you tell anyone else about what you'd found?" Myles asked.

"No, though my son-in-law seemed quite interested in what I was doing. He's always had a curiosity about the art of my family. I think he expects to inherit the shop one day. Too bad he has no skills when it comes to working with his hands."

Myles didn't want to alarm the old man as to his son-in-law's possible involvement in Cheesecake's dognapping. He'd been so helpful. "Do you think we could talk to your son-in-law? If he showed an interest, he might know some other places to search."

"You're quite taken with that little bobble, aren't you? There's nothing that makes a craftsman prouder than to know something he's made is cherished. Pierre must be resting just a little bit easier right now. I can't imagine what you'd find out from Link. I love my daughter and respect her choice for a husband, but that guy will never measure up in my eyes. He drives limos around town. I'll get you his information."

~

Between investigative forays with Myles, working at the coffee shop, and her weekly performance with Polly Urethane and the Strippers, it took the better part of a week for Kendell to find a quiet day off for some quality time with Cheesecake. Her dog was feeling better, but she still yipped, barked, and made running motions with her feet as she slept. More than once, Kendell had woken her up because she seemed to be having a nightmare. Each time, the old dog gave her a lick or two of appreciation before rolling over to once again try and conquer her world of sleep. Neither of them had managed an uninterrupted eight hours since the rescue.

Kendell pulled Cecile, her whitewood acoustic guitar, from her case and began playing "You've Got a Friend." Making music on the old instrument was more a collaboration than a performance. Her fingers tapped on the strings like she was performing a gentle massage. Each note was like the soft voice of someone she'd known since her earliest days learning to play—those once harsh stumbling sounds now smooth and effortless.

The song's lyrics never failed to call Cheesecake to her side. The dog jumped onto the couch and laid her head on Kendell's leg to look up at her mistress's mouth and fingers, where the wonderful sounds came from.

Kendell's eyes misted as she saw Cheesecake returning to the sweet, lazy dog, indicating that everything was good in their world. No matter what went on outside the apartment, they had each other. Not even a curse could change that bond.

The smell of sugar cookies wafted in from the kitchen.

Kendell had never known a guy not to revert back to being a little boy when given a batch of baked goods, and cookies shaped like her dog were Kendell's favorite to make.

Cheesecake gave her the familiar look of suspicion as the timer went off.

Kendell set her guitar aside. "It's not like that. We still owe him some kind of thanks for coming to our rescue. Since when have you known me to make the first move on a guy? It's not like my domestic skills have ever impressed anyone. I promise you he won't get the wrong impression. If he hasn't tried to make a move on me by now, I doubt he ever will. Guys just aren't that clever."

But she knew her dog had a point even if she didn't want to admit it. Myles wasn't like any other guy she'd met. The fact that she'd called him that night and not Polly or one of her other friends still baffled her. Looking back, he had seemed the most logical choice. He knew about the pipe tool. He kept late hours because of his job as a bartender. And, well, he was a guy. She felt safe around him. But her actions that night weren't based on logic. In her terror, he'd been the one she wanted by her side. "Okay, so I'll only give him half the batch. Will that make you feel better?"

Cheesecake could be a tough customer when it came to seeing Kendell losing control of her emotions. As a loyal companion, she preferred a quiet domicile where she was Kendell's only confidant. Unwanted visitors, men in particular, had to earn their way into Cheesecake's good graces and prove themselves worthy of Kendell's affections.

DAYS WOULD PASS between Myles's opportunities to pursue the investigation with Kendell. He resented the breaks. There was so much work to be done. As he nibbled at one of the few remaining cookies with white-and-black frosting, he checked himself in his hall mirror. He shouldn't care what he looked like for her. She was still more like a best friend's sister than anything else. But memories of seeing her in her short skirt behind her electric guitar, playing to all of the audience's desires, had a way of infecting his nightly dreams. The fact that she challenged him mentally didn't hurt either. Unlike Charlie and his desire to fuck any woman who didn't know any better, Myles had prided himself on wanting to get to know a woman first. Not that he had such intentions with Kendell. He made a quick check of his hands and clothes to make sure he was presentable for their next research project.

He shivered at entering the Williams Research Center building of the Historic New Orleans Collection. "This place reminds me of school."

Kendell, however, was in her element. "I know, right? I love it here."

"I think you and I had very different school experiences."

Their online research had failed to uncover any mention of the baron Malveaux other than what Mr. Boudreaux had already told them. Myles figured the man and his deeds had been lost to history. Though he knew of libraries and research facilities like this one, he'd never bothered to set foot in one. Even the most complex of his college papers had relied almost exclusively on what he could pull up on his laptop.

As Kendell explained their mission to the woman at the desk—who looked exactly like a caricature of someone's grandmother—he surveyed the ornately carved shelves filled with books. In his mind, he heard his mother telling him to look but not touch.

The old woman struggled to her feet. "I'll get you set up over here. The rules are clearly displayed. Almost all of our documents are very old and fragile. Please, do be careful."

He thought she fit that description herself. As the woman disappeared into the stacks, Kendell pulled out her writing pad and a pencil. Myles couldn't remember using writing implements since he was a little kid. "You have got to be kidding me."

"It's all they allow in here. Some documents we can get photocopied, but most of the information we're looking for is too delicate." She gave him an appraising stare. "Maybe it'd be best if you just looked over my shoulder."

It was all he could do to keep from making a snarky response. But the truth was that he didn't really want to be responsible for handling something of historical significance. "What did she find?"

"Mostly newspaper articles. Apparently, the baron was very involved in high society, so his name pops up each time there was some big event. She thinks there are some old photographs of the Malveaux mansion and maybe even some of the family. Sitting here is like waiting for Santa Claus."

"More like Mrs. Claus." Though really he saw it as closer to waiting on some elementary school teacher to show him how badly he'd messed up.

He had a momentary urge to rush up and help the old curator as she struggled toward their table carrying a mammoth ledger filled with brittle yellow newspapers. But the prospect of damaging either the woman or the documents kept him riveted in place.

She set the huge book in front of Kendell. "Take your time. I do trust you, dear, but these are older than most of the documents you usually request. Handle them carefully."

Kendell looked up like a little girl just entrusted with her mother's diamond necklace. "I will."

The old woman gave him the hint of a hard stare as she returned to her desk. He realized how out of his depth he was as Kendell put on a pair of white cotton gloves. Carefully, she opened the front cover to reveal a paper from July 10, 1843. The yellowed page, though undoubtedly historic, didn't look especially informative.

"Are we going to have to go through every page?" The best he'd ever been able to manage with the Sunday paper was the cartoons.

"No, Edith said the date we're looking for is August 2." Kendell continued to turn each page with reverence.

"That'd be, like, a quarter of the way through the ledger. Why not just flip to that section?"

She gave him a look of exasperation. "First of all, because we might miss something important. Secondly, because that's not how to handle old paper."

For a moment, he thought she was going to tell him to sit at the table and draw her a pretty picture while she did her research. He decided it'd be best to just look over her shoulder in silence.

According to the clock above the door, it took Kendell fourteen minutes to reach the page in question. And once there, they found that the obituary for Serephine Malveaux only occupied a single paragraph. For a family as famous as the baron's, very little was said about the passing of his "beloved daughter." Even the cause of death had been ignored.

"Looks like he got to the reporter." Kendell ran her cotton-covered finger over the notification.

"Why do you say that?"

She moved to the next column. "Look at the other obituaries. They all list some horrible form of death. Serephine's is filled with glowing remembrances but no facts. Even back then, I suspect suicide wasn't something a powerful family would want broadcast."

For someone who hadn't studied history, she had a remarkable way of seeing behind the cover story. It was a skill he'd never really mastered even as an archeology student. "It's still not proof that what I saw was real."

"True, but it's also not a repudiation. I'll have Edith get us those photographs." She squinted at him. "Don't touch anything."

"Yes, *Mom.*" He watched her as she walked down the line of tables. *Sexy library-loving nerd.*

He sat in the seat she'd vacated to read the rest of the page that lay open. Serephine's mother and father had given heartfelt, if not a little flowery, proclamations of their bereavement. The words looked overly polished for parents who'd just lost their daughter. Perhaps Kendell was right. If the girl had committed suicide, the family would have been careful in what they said. Her brother, Antoine-Caliste Malveaux, however, was only quoted as saying, "Rest easy, sweet Sere. I will never forget." Myles wrote the words down in Kendell's notebook.

"You haven't been touching that newspaper have you?"

"No, ma'am." He turned to see Kendell smiling down at him. "That wasn't nice."

She failed to contain her giggle. "Sorry. I couldn't resist."

The curator had an easier time with the book of family photographs. "We're in luck. This album dates from 1902, so I originally missed it. The second half is from the family Laurette, but the first half is all Malveaux, dating back to the early 1800s. There's no explanation for the change of family, but after the War Between the States, people used whatever they could find to display photographs. There's a sizable missing period of time that corresponds to the war. Often those pictures were kept in a separate album or removed entirely."

Of the possible explanations, a marriage between the Malveaux and Laurette families seemed the most plausible to Myles, though he also jotted down that adoption, war buddies, and extended family inheritance were possible reasons for the mixed family photo album.

Kendell opened the engraved leather cover. A faded photograph of a mansion with live oaks on either side filled the front page. If it weren't for the out-of-focus horse-drawn trolley that blurred the lower right edge of the picture, he would have thought the house was on a plantation. The inscription at the bottom of the page read, "Malveaux Estate on Saint Charles, 1821"

As she slowly flipped the pages, he got the pictorial representation of a youth born to privilege. Archibald Baptiste Malveaux had the smug countenance of young man who'd never known economic suffering. For the first handful of pages, his parents, who looked so old they could have passed as his grandparents, were constantly photographed with Archibald between them. By the time they disappeared from the pictures, the young aristocrat had already been joined by a lovely woman who appeared slightly uncomfortable in the trappings of her husband's wealth. Myles had to remind himself not to read too much into the pictures.

The couple only appeared alone together for a couple of pages before a baby filled the woman's arms. Her expensive necklaces and flowing gowns were quickly replaced by more utilitarian attire. As their son, Antoine-Caliste, grew, he managed a more unpretentious though no less intense countenance than his father. Though it was clear his mother doted on Antoine, Archibald continued his cold stare of command.

Myles guessed Antoine to be just shy of his teenage years when a baby girl joined the family. Even the cold facial expressions of Archibald—now simply referred to as "the baron"—softened as he rested his hand on his wife's shoulder. His eyes no longer bore into the camera but instead rested on the child in her mother's arms.

As the girl outgrew her mother's lap, she took her place in front of her gangly brother, standing between their parents. Other than young Serephine, it appeared the family didn't care much for each other. With each new page of the album, Antoine's posture appeared more reserved, his arms crossed, and he gave no notice of his parents. If Myles hadn't known better, he would have thought the boy had been edited into the pictures.

"He's quite striking." Kendell had stopped turning the pages.

"The baron? He kind of looks like an asshole to me."

She pointed at a picture without touching it. "No. Antoine. There's a soulful pain in his eyes. He must be in his midteens here, but his expressions are much more mature. It's like he's carrying a heavy emotional burden."

Myles leaned in for a better look. From the youth's muscle tone and stance, he clearly knew how to handle himself, but he never smiled for any of the pictures. Myles reminded himself that smiling for the camera wasn't the norm in the 1800s. "I think that's just the way people posed back then."

Kendell frowned at him. "I'm well aware of how people presented themselves for portraits. In some ways, their stoicism makes it easier to read what they were thinking. There's no pretend happiness to mask their eyes. Look at the difference between father and son. They have the same features, but you can tell what they're thinking is very different."

He did his best to see what she meant, but he couldn't empirically conclude that the impression was just what she wanted to see. "Turn the page. Maybe we can tell more about him as he grows up."

But the next dozen pages were only frayed edges where the paper had been torn. Kendell ran her gloved finger over the soft, uneven edges. "This must be the Civil War years. I wonder if they tore them out because Antoine served in the Confederate army or if it was because he died and they didn't want to be reminded. Someone must have suffered a lot to try and remove the memories that way."

This time, he could see her point. It would have been easier to just take out the pictures, or if they'd really wanted the whole pages removed, a knife or scissors would have done a cleaner job. From the torn edges, it looked more like someone had pulled them out in a fit of rage. "They probably wouldn't have told us much anyway. In those last photographs, Serephine looked pretty close to the age I imagined her while holding the tool."

Kendell leaned back in the chair to face him. "Do you think that's why the pages were ripped out? Her suicide had to be difficult on the family. Even if they stuck together after her death, their relationships were probably strained. It'd be easy to imagine that at some point something else went wrong. Maybe the baron and his wife divorced, and whoever tore at these pages concluded Serephine's death was the beginning of their woes."

"Sounds a little overly sentimental to me. Turn to the next section. I can't help but believe there's some connection between the Malveaux family and the Laurettes."

Pictures of the Laurette family weren't as posed as the Malveaux portraits. Post-Civil War photography had a more realistic nature, or at least, that was the case for the Laurette family. The first few pictures almost looked randomly compiled. What people there were in the images were engaged in either surveying property or doing their daily tasks. Though not as wealthy as the Malveauxs, the Laurette photographs still displayed a family investing in rebuilding New Orleans.

It took Kendell flipping through five pages before they found the first image of Anthony Laurette, the founding member of Laurette and Associates Architecture. Myles immediately noticed why the man had been missing from earlier photographs. His scraggly beard insufficiently hid an ugly scar that ran from his forehead, under an eye patch, and down below his left ear. Myles had difficulty guessing the man's age. His hair was still dark in the yellowed photos, but from his stooped posture, he easily could have been approaching middle age.

Myles lost sight of the picture when Kendell grabbed her magnifying glass and dove into the album.

"I was looking at that."

"Hush a minute. There's something familiar about this guy."

He'd seen enough Civil War photographs to know every one of those soldiers looked both eerily familiar and completely foreign at the same time.

She leaned back into her chair and scowled. "I must be suffering from your affliction of not knowing what's real and what I'm imagining."

"What do you think you saw?"

She handed him the magnifying glass. "Look at his good eye. Nothing else, just the eye. And don't touch the photograph."

"I know. You've told me enough times. I'll be careful of the damn precious historical treasures."

In spite of his promise, he found it difficult to lean in without touching the oversized album. "He's only got one eye, so any comparison would be a challenge. But I assume you're going to tell me he's got similar features to Antoine Malveaux. It's not unlikely that they were related. After all, this album does have pictures of both families."

Carefully, Kendell turned the pages back to the final image of the Malveaux family. "I don't think they're related. I think they're the same person. I wasn't looking at the shape of his eye but that look of intensity. Imagine this young man going through the Civil War and coming out the other end as the beaten soldier."

Looking at only the right eye, Myles had to really squint to make anything out of the family photograph. "That's a real stretch, Kendell. Why would he change his name? If he wanted to change his identity, the last place he'd go after the war would be to New Orleans where his father was so well known."

"All I'm saying is look at his eyes."

He had her flip back to Anthony Laurette and tried to imagine him being only ten years older than the teenaged Antoine. War, especially that one, did leave marks on people that went much further than skin deep. "Let's keep going through the album. Maybe we'll see some other indication."

But the farther Kendell flipped through the historical reference, the less Mr. Laurette, the famous architect who stood proudly in front of so many Garden District mansions, resembled the gangly son of the baron Malveaux.

9

*T*hough Kendell often got talked into attending the big Mardi Gras parades, it was the smaller ones that took place a good month before Fat Tuesday that she truly enjoyed. She wandered around the staging park for the Krewe of Barkus, looking at all the participants. Cheesecake kept close to her side as Kendell pushed the old bicycle with the front basket. Her pretty girl always stood a little straighter after a wash and haircut. This year's theme was Dogs in Entertainment. Even though not the correct breed or hair color, Cheesecake would make the perfect Toto with Kendell playing the supporting role of Dorothy.

Being part of the parade allowed them access to the Barkus pre-pawty, where everyone gathered to enjoy the spectacle before the official parade through the French Quarter. Cheesecake had her unique way of greeting and expressing her appreciation for her fellow dogs' costumes. She barked playfully at a small dog and his companion dressed up as a box of Cracker Jacks. Astro and his Jetson family received a howl of delight. The Bat Hound decked out in cape and mask elicited a growl of suspicion. Cheesecake warmed up when instead of a powerful Batman, the dog's accomplice turned out to be a Batgirl not much younger than Kendell. The sight of Cujo, however, made Cheesecake pull Kendell to the other side of the park.

There never was much order to the Barkus parade, but Kendell did her best to find a spot with her fellow on-screen characters. The best she could manage was a mother and daughter with a shaggy dog they insisted on calling Paul Anka and a small pug dog with his companion wearing an all-black suit and dark glasses. Even starting at the back of the line, Kendell knew she'd have to pedal the bike slowly to avoid rushing to the front of the slow-moving procession.

From behind, she saw Bat Hound join the ranks of Blue Dog, Underdog, and Scooby Doo. As was nearly always the case with these parades, the nearest thing to being organized was waiting for the organizers to open the gates.

Revelers lined the route, cheering on every dog and their human attendant. Kendell reached forward to pet Cheesecake, who rode proudly in the bike's basket. Other dogs would have to walk the streets, getting their paws dirty in the drinks people carelessly spilled. Cheesecake rode above the random attention from the ill-behaved crowd and unruly breeds. Though not the queen of the parade, she gazed on her admirers with regal appreciation.

As the loud procession rounded the corner to Chartres Street, what little discipline the parade had attempted broke down. A little girl dressed as Lisa Simpson lost control of her puppy dressed as Santa's Little Helper. The athletic dog took off after a larger, shaggy dog being escorted by an old man in a white lab coat and crazy white hair. The large dog nearly ran into Kendell. Her only warning was the man's yell of, "Einstein!"

Kendell managed to reach down and grab the leather leash that snaked along beside her bike. Cheesecake barked her displeasure at the undignified manner in which some dogs insisted on participating in what was clearly *her* parade. Fortunately, the fracas didn't last long as the people lining the street were only too happy to distract the unruly dogs from their misadventure.

The old man dressed as Doc Brown took the leash from Kendell. "Thanks for rescuing my dog. I'm afraid he gets spooked by so much attention."

Even under the crazy wig that fell in the man's face, Kendell recognized the penetrating deep-blue eyes. "Professor Yates?"

The man's laugh confirmed her suspicion. "No one has called me that for some time. Which class did I make you suffer through?"

"The Transfer of Human Energy into Inanimate Objects."

Regaining control of his dog proved easier than persuading the creature to return to the parade. The big guy seemed far too intent on getting attention from the girl, who'd once again reined in her jumpy brown mutt. It took Professor Yates pulling a dog treat out from his pocket to bribe Einstein back into the procession. "I remember that class. I only taught it a couple of times—never could get it accepted into a college curriculum. Have you been keeping up with your research?"

Kendell wanted to tell him everything she and Myles had been up to, but a parade didn't seem the ideal location for a chat. "Would it surprise you to find that I had?"

"Not at all. People attract what they want to learn. If you found that class in spite of all the institution's attempts at squashing it, other means of understanding would likely follow."

His odd way of talking forced her to pay attention. Cheesecake, however, began barking at her fellow canines, who clearly weren't taking the parade seriously enough for her tastes. Defecating on the route was just bad form. "I think I'd better get her ahead of some of these less-well-behaved marchers."

He reached under his lab coat and pulled out a business card. "I don't want to interrupt your fun. You can find me around Jackson Square most weekends."

As he hurried off under the tug of his big dog, she had a quick look at the card, which read, "Scientific Psychic Readings."

MYLES WONDERED why some mistakes simply refused to stay in the past where they belonged. Kendell searched the face of each mystic who conned money out of passing tourists. He hoped she wouldn't find the fake professor. The stupid class where he'd first met her had been nothing but a waste of time and money. Not that he felt much different about half of the college courses that actually had been sanctioned by the university, but at least those had gotten him a few credits closer to graduation. The Transfer of Human Energy into Inanimate Objects hadn't even added a single credit, according to his academic advisor. All he'd gotten from his advisor's research on the course was her laugh of derision.

Kendell pointed to a dark corner away from the gypsy-looking characters with their brightly colored tables. "I think that's him over there. See the guy in the steampunk outfit?"

Perfect. The man in the long black coat, leather top hat, and round glasses looked exactly like a snake-oil salesman. "Don't you think he's already swindled enough money out of us?"

She nudged him playfully as she ate the praline he'd bought for her. "We have the upper hand this time. He only thinks he knows what he's talking about. We may not have proof yet, but at least we're not trying to capitalize on people's imaginations."

"You made it." The man's smile reminded Myles of a spider who'd just noticed an insect had stumbled into its web.

Kendell motioned to Myles. "I brought a friend who also took that class. We have a few questions, if we're not interrupting your workday."

The fake professor made a show of removing his coat to reveal a Victorian waistcoat printed in purple fleur-de-lis on a black background. "Please, have a seat."

Myles figured his best course of action was to take

charge of the dialogue. "I can accept that your course was designed to make us consider the unusual. So many curricula only study what is already established. But do you believe what you taught? Have you experienced any of it, or was it all just speculation?"

"Straight to the point. I remember you well, Mr. Garrison. As an answer, would you allow me to do a reading on you? Free of charge of course."

Myles doubted anything the man did was truly without strings. But at least if he paid for the service, it would be a one-time cost. He took a seat in front of the high-backed white-and-gold chair with Kendell by his side. "What would that involve?"

The supposed fortune-teller reached into his cabinet on wheels and pulled out a device that looked equal parts antique medical eye-examination equipment and steampunk tomfoolery. Myles leaned back in his chair to keep as clear of the headgear as possible. "I assure you it's perfectly safe. You lean against the chin support. The goggles read your eye movements as the computer screen displays various images that change depending on where you focus. I'll ask you a series of questions while I place items in your hand."

Sounds exactly like what a carnival charlatan would say. "And this thing isn't going to shoot acid into my eyes or electrocute me or something?"

"I haven't been prosecuted yet."

The headgear covered Myles's eyes. Matching steampunk-decorated headphones fit so tightly around his ears he could barely make out the brass band a block away.

The man's voice came through like a doctor safely protected from his experiment. "Let your eyes relax. The idea is for you to react without thinking. I'll start by putting you into a mild trance."

"I'm not crazy about the idea of being hypnotized." The last thing he wanted was to end up dancing naked in Jackson Square, or worse, in Saint Louis Cathedral.

"I don't put you that deep. Just look into the spinning vortex. This is only meant to relax your mind, not influence you in any way."

The calm, disembodied voice nicely matched the slow-moving spinning disk. Myles didn't feel sleepy. It was more like he'd had a pint of well-crafted microbrew. The image switched to four views of the sky in different weather conditions. His eyes drifted to the sunny day. Four new images appeared. He chose a big shaggy dog, which ran in a meadow, complementing the sunny-day image.

"These first tests are just to calibrate my equipment to you. I'm putting this tennis ball in your hand. Tell me what you feel."

He had an urge to throw it to see how the dog on the screen would react. "It's warm, but I'd guess that was because you kept it out in the sun." He suspected most suckers who sat in the chair would believe they were experiencing something more significant.

"Very perceptive. Let's try something else."

The images and objects varied from homey and peaceful to dark and threatening, but with each change, Myles knew his reactions were being manipulated. Even with all the gear, the man just wasn't that subtle in setting up the mental scenes.

"Fuck! Ouch, that hurt." Myles's pulling away from the strange contraption accompanied the clanking of the knife to the ground.

The man's eyes bored into Myles. "What did you feel?"

"It burned the palm of my hand. You really need to watch the temperature setting of your warming oven."

Kendell took his hand. "I don't see any marks."

The man picked up the knife and ran it across his own palm. "This one wasn't a con. I do warm and cool other objects, it's true. But we moved beyond that calibration. The image you were looking at had been overlaid with a blue lens. In case you didn't notice, with each answer you gave me, the eyepiece changed color to slightly influence your next set of images. For a person with normal abilities, their answers while they hold the knife are typically 'dark, foreboding, and dangerous.' You're the first to feel actual pain. Fascinating."

Myles didn't think it was *fascinating* at all. In fact, he still expected blisters to start appearing on his palm. "And what does this experiment tell you, *Professor*?"

Professor Yates wiped the knife blade clean and set it on a piece of velvet. "Miss Summer, would you touch the blade to prove that it's not dangerous?"

Myles wanted to stop her, but Kendell didn't hesitate in running her fingers over the gleaming steal. "It just feels like a knife to me."

The man motioned to Myles. "Your turn."

Myles figured that whatever the man had done to

prepare the blade, the effect must have worn off. But to his dismay, he could still only barely touch the thing. "Well, it's not searing my flesh off, but I swear it still feels hot."

"Interesting. The visual stimulations and mild hypnotic state were meant to heighten any psychometric abilities you might have without allowing the object to unduly influence your thoughts. That's why it seemed hotter while we were conducting the experiment. That knife was used in a stabbing recently. I won't tell you how I came to possess it. I need to protect my sources of useful artifacts. You're the first person to properly identify that past energy. Have you experienced anything like this before?"

Myles said nothing, but Kendell dove into their history with the pipe tool as well as his discovery of the World War II airplane.

The man looked lost in thought as he put his fingers together at his chin. "So you no longer have the item?"

Myles started to worry he'd have to touch everything with a degree of caution. "Like she said, it was stolen."

"In my experience, things that have a destiny tend to end up circling back around to the people they're meant to find. Should you run across the pipe tool again, I'd be interested in seeing it. I might be able to provide you more answers if I were in physical contact with the item."

10

*K*endell held her breath as Myles cinched up her black leather bustier. Her white cotton blouse billowed at the sleeves and waist. Her breasts felt two cups larger from the stiff garment. "Thanks for helping out." She enjoyed making him blush.

"The day I don't accept a friend's invitation to help dress a group of hot ladies for their Mardi Gras parade is the day I know I'm dead."

A smattering of laughter went up around the section of parking lot designated for last-minute wardrobe adjustments. Asking him to assist with her pirate outfit had really only been an excuse to have him close by. "I love my Krewe of Muses sisters, but these floats still make my skin crawl. I keep expecting to see one of Cheesecake's abductors lurking around. At least I didn't have to go back to that fucking warehouse to join the parade."

He escorted her down the row of marching bands,

revelers, and brightly decorated floats. His hand at her back gave her a degree of comfort. "I know what you mean. If your dog had joined us, she might be a little spun up right now. Just focus on the theme of the parade."

She smiled back at him. The Krewe of Muses' organizers had picked the theme of the parade, Damsels No Longer in Distress, months earlier, but the name couldn't be more apt now that Kendell had her dog back. The swashbuckling female pirate crew, who the previous night had been playing at the Scratchy Dog as Polly Urethane and the Strippers, would be having a grand time atop the pirate ship float. The only men allowed in the procession were defeated villains. Not to Kendell's surprise, Myles had turned down the request to pose as the pirates' captured and humiliated English Lord. As he helped her up the ladder, she wished he didn't have to leave.

He must have seen her look of concern. "You've got your girls with you. And if you feel unsafe or see someone that makes you uncomfortable, call me. I'll have your scooter stashed nearby so I can get to you faster than you might suspect. Otherwise, I'll see you on Canal Street."

She knew her anxiety was foolish. No one in their right mind would try anything during a parade with so many people watching, but her emotions seldom listened to logic. "I'll throw you something special." She gave him a wink she hoped would hide her fear.

Being above the action was a position Kendell preferred, but as the tractor lurched forward, she nearly fell against Polly and her bag of rubber-sword throws. "This is going to be a bumpy ride."

"Good thing we're not trying to play our music up here. Though we could use the publicity." Polly was always on the lookout for free advertisement.

As the parade turned onto Napoleon to form up behind the Krewe of Chaos, Kendell got into the spirit of the event. People were shouting in anticipation as she lifted a handful of bead strands from the bag at her feet and threw them high into the air. She tried to aim for the kids. At this point in the route, enough families were represented that any swag the children didn't catch was often handed over to them by a caring adult. The same would not be true as they approached the French Quarter.

Minerva tossed doubloons from her purple, gold, and green sequined purse like some demented sexy fairy godmother. "I have more fun up on these floats than down there watching the parades. If grown men only knew how ridiculous they look jumping and screaming like little kids at Halloween."

The tractor slowed to a stop so the marching band behind their pirate ship float could get fully into their rendition of Fleetwood Mac's "Tusk." The mostly instrumental number made Kendell break into a dance atop the float with the other members of her band while those around the edge tried to moderate how many beads and cups they tossed to the crowd. "At this rate, it'll take all day to get to the Canal Street."

"You in a hurry?" Minerva asked.

Kendell kicked the brightly decorated handbag she'd stashed under the wooden bench. "No. I just want to see

Myles's face when he sees me up here. I plan on making all the women go crazy around him."

She opened the bag to show Minerva the bead strands with pictures of Myles circled by the words "Kiss This Guy for Me."

"You're a saucy minx. Just remember, he did save your ass."

Ahead of them, a tractor pulled a float decorated as an old-time steam train with the villain tied to the front. From her perch above the crowd, Kendell saw the driver miss his turn and slam on the breaks to avoid veering into the barricade. She just had time to grab the railing before the pirate ship also abruptly came to a stop. "What the hell?"

Their tractor driver waved his walkie-talkie that was used to coordinate the various floats. Being so close to the tail end of one float ahead, with limited vision in the front, often meant drivers had to take quick action. "Sounds like there was a tire blowout that caused a tractor to miss the turn. We'll be sitting here for a bit while they get everything untangled."

Down on the street, the security ushers who kept the crowd behind the barricades rushed toward the broken-down float to offer assistance. *Great. Now we really will be here all day.* But before her irritation could truly settle in, she felt her cell phone vibrate.

She could barely hear Myles over the crowd noise that surrounded them both. "You okay?"

"Sure. It was just a breakdown." News must have traveled faster than she expected.

She heard the concern in his voice. "I'm right in front of

the railway float. Looks like someone was hurt when it stopped so unexpectedly. The medics raced back from the Krewe of Chaos. I'm going to work my way back to you."

When Kendell turned to Polly for some official explanation, she saw that her bandleader was white as a sheet. She nearly dropped her sequined cell phone.

"I've got a friend on that float," Polly said. "She said someone got stabbed. You should get down and mix in with the crowd. It sounds like it was an accident. One of their members was making a show of cleaning the villain's pipe when the knife slipped and went into her neck as the float jerked to a halt. My friend says there's a lot of blood. She was nearly hysterical."

It didn't take much imagination for Kendell to envision the scene complete with that damn pipe tool as the murder weapon—though the line between homicide and accident was pretty obscure when a cursed item was involved. "I'll wait for Myles to get here. There's no reason to panic, but I think you're right. I'd just as soon not be around if people start asking questions."

MYLES KNEW the city would have procedures in place for the inevitable float mishap. Between the million people on vacation, and the congested streets filled with people struggling to catch some useless piece of plastic, and the revelry, which often involved too much alcohol, he was amazed people didn't get hurt more often. But his sense of panic didn't come from the claustrophobia of so many partiers pressed around him. As he scanned the float for the injured individual, he spotted Samantha Laurette trembling next to a uniformed cop on the street. Her outfit of flowing, turn-of-the-century skirt and white blouse made it clear she'd been one of the people on the float.

As he approached, he heard the policeman talking to her. "There's nothing more for you to do. The medics will get her to the hospital. Do you have anyone who could take you home?"

He couldn't make out from her quivering if she was shaking her head or in a state of shock.

"Officer, I know Miss Laurette. I can escort her home if she'd like."

Samantha nodded her agreement as she turned to Myles. "Thank you. This has all been quite a shock."

The policeman jotted down Myles's information. The exercise seemed completely pointless, but he guessed the officer had a procedure to follow.

Myles kept hold of her hand as they weaved their way through the dense crowd. As they approached Kendell's pirate ship, he pulled out his cell phone, which he carried at her request, and texted her, "Meet me at the coffee shop on the corner."

Though the people vied for every available foot of real estate along the parade route, the shops often were eerily quiet. Tourists couldn't catch strands of cheap beads inside businesses that were trying to generate income for their employees. Even with the parade at a standstill, revelers would spend their time harassing members stranded on the floats in an attempt to get the shiniest baubles rather than take the time to find food. Starts and stops were unpredictable, and few people wanted to miss what might be coming around the corner.

The barista smiled at Myles as he ordered three large coffees. "Another breakdown this early in the day? With the other parades still to come, it'll be midnight before the streets are clear."

He felt sorry for the haggard woman behind the counter. "Getting to and from work must be a pain."

"All part of living in New Orleans. Have a seat anywhere, and I'll bring you your coffees when they're ready."

He put an extra couple of dollars in the tip jar and directed Samantha to a discreet corner table of the café.

Kendell squeezed past the crowd outside into the café just as the coffee arrived. She looked less shocked than he would have thought on seeing Samantha, but then, his partner always was fast when it came to figuring things out. "What happened?"

The woman was still shaking, but as she looked around to make sure they wouldn't be overheard he knew she wanted someone to confide in. "Marilyn is a distant cousin. I barely know her. I think she felt bad that I had to clean out my grandparents' house alone, so she got me into the parade even though getting on a float is nearly impossible. I knew her choosing that pipe-cleaning tool was a mistake. When we saw it as part of the float costume paraphernalia, I nearly called you. But I figured you must have lost interest in it, or worse, had some misfortune and got rid of it. Accidents seem to follow that thing around."

Myles watched her closely for her response. "Actually, it was stolen from us."

Samantha took a deep breath. Her quivering exhalation let him know she was less shocked than concerned. "Do you have any clues as to who took it?"

"We think they work at Float World. How random was it that your cousin picked out the tool? I would have thought the thieves wouldn't have left it lying around."

She closed her eyes and shook her head. "I don't think it was random at all. Someone intended for her to pick it up. We get to choose our own costumes from what the organizers lay out, but some items naturally go together. The Sherlock pipe, tool, and Victorian villain's hat were set next to a flowing purple dress. It was just the type of character and outfit Marilyn would be drawn to."

Kendell set her coffee cup down with slow deliberation. "You think her injury was intentional?"

"It wasn't an accident, and it wasn't an injury. I know enough about medicine to know a punctured neck artery when I see one. Blood was spurting out all over the locomotive's cabin. The medics didn't want to alarm anyone, especially me, but if Marilyn makes it through the night, I'll be amazed. I should have gone to the hospital, but the family's put enough of a burden on me without me also having to be the one to make the phone calls of doom. I gave the medics her information so they'll know who to call. I just want to get the hell out of this city. My father was right. This place has it in for anyone in the Laurette family."

Finding a cursed item from over a hundred and fifty

years ago and using it as a means of committing murder seemed a little farfetched. "Was there someone after her?"

"You sound like a detective. Maybe we should go to the police with what I know, but I can't imagine they'd listen. Marilyn is a reporter down here. She mostly writes about high-society events and interesting historical tidbits. I'm sure there will be an investigation, but with so many witnesses seeing the tractor's tire blow out and her stab herself with the knife, it's not likely the case will go very far."

Kendell started tapping out some notes on her phone. "If you don't know who murdered her, and you believe it was intentional, you must know more about the pipe tool than you originally told us."

Samantha stared down into her coffee and bit her lip. He suspected she was either creating some clever cover story or deciding how much to divulge. Considering her emotional state, he chose to give her the benefit of the doubt. "The Laurette name is well known down here, as are all the branches of the family. As I mentioned at the house, my grandfather had a passion for documenting the family tree. I did find his writings by the way. They were kept in a couple of shoe boxes under his bed. When I was young, I thought his ramblings were just the foolishness of an old man trying to find meaning in his life through association with those of the past. But when my father took up the cause and started investigating how each person had died, I suspected there was something he wasn't telling me. It was only when Dad knew he was dying and I'd inherit the house that he gave me the diary."

Kendell nearly dropped her coffee cup. "Whose diary? What did it say? Can we see it?"

Samantha shook her head. "It's still in Atlanta. Dad made it clear that he didn't want it coming back to New Orleans. He said I'd be in enough danger as it was. He's also the one who warned me against admitting to knowing anything about the Malveaux family. I'm sorry I hid that from you, but you had just walked in off the street."

Kendell reached out to take her hand. "I guess we were pretty presumptuous knocking on your door and asking about your family like that. We're trying to make sense out of what we've discovered. If we're prying, just say so, and we'll leave you alone."

Samantha's smile looked forced. "I could use someone who isn't a part of my family to talk to. But I'm afraid the diary won't be as helpful as you'd like. It was the war journal of my ancestor, Anthony Laurette. It left me with more questions than answers. He did know Antoine-Caliste Malveaux. According to Anthony, he died early in the war. Anthony described him as an athletic youth, but other than that one attribute, he was completely unfit for battle. He said that in spite of the boy's privileged upbringing, he was too compassionate for the horrors of war. Apparently, in their first skirmish Antoine ran out of the tree line into a volley of musket fire."

Myles tried to hide his disappointment. "It doesn't sound like they knew each other for long."

"That's one of the confusing aspects of the diary. It's clear Antoine died within the first two pages of the journal, but for the rest of the book, Anthony has many conversations with the deceased Antoine. Dad believed Anthony either suffered from bouts of delusions or a dissociative identity disorder—multiple personalities."

The excitement in Kendell's voice was unmistakable. "He thought Anthony and Antoine were the same person?"

Myles took a sip of his coffee, grateful she hadn't said, "I told you so."

The more Samantha talked about the past, the calmer her voice sounded. "War does strange things to people. It's impossible to know just from the one diary what Anthony's state of mind was when he wrote the passages. If you believe them to be the same person, he didn't see how he could endure the war or his past. Antoine's death—be it physical or psychological—forever changed Anthony."

Questions were floating around Myles's head like the buzz of the tourists hurrying to the next parade. "Did he say anything about Antoine's sister Serephine?"

"Yes. Their first conversation after Antoine's supposed death revolved around the Malveaux family. Apparently, his sister died in their father's office with the door and windows bolted shut from the inside. It was quickly ruled a suicide, but Antoine didn't accept that. He said Serephine was too full of life to end hers so young. There was never an explanation that I could find, but Antoine blamed his father. Clearly, there was some family falling-out even before Serephine's death."

Myles focused on his breathing to avoid jumping to conclusions. What he'd seen matched up nicely with Samantha's account so far. "Was there any mention of how she killed herself?"

"You want me to tell you it was that pipe tool you found, but the journal wasn't that specific. Antoine referred to a pocketknife that was too dull to accomplish the deed as being the only sharp object found next to his dead sister."

Kendell tapped her fingers against her coffee cup. "But it could have been the pipe tool. I'm still unclear on why your dad was so concerned about the diary."

Samantha took a deep breath and let it out slowly. "About halfway through the diary—not long after the battle of Fort Jackson but before the fall of New Orleans—they had a conversation regarding 'Anthony's grand obligation.' The title came up numerous times after this conversation. Antoine said his father, the baron Malveaux, was a truly evil man, and every family member including the extended family must be forever alert to unseen dangers. But only those of legitimate descent from the baron would be in direct peril. You have to realize, Anthony was writing this after a big battle that the South lost. He had to know New Orleans was about to fall. His mind wasn't all there."

Myles could see Samantha was having trouble believing the story herself, but having someone die in front of her was far more convincing than a hundred-and-fifty-year-old diary. "You think he was referring to a family curse?"

"If it were just me, I'd put it down to an overactive imagination. My grandfather was nearly a recluse toward the end of his life. He was convinced he would meet with some accident if he set foot outside the door. Dad's research on how our ancestors died was pretty speculative in my opinion. I mean, everyone dies somehow. Antoine warned Anthony to be on the lookout for any of the baron's personal artifacts. He said they would be everyday objects. Things the baron might have carried with him. That's why Dad had me read the diary before he died. He was worried I'd find something in that house that would cause a family member's death or my own."

"And yet he left you the house." Myles couldn't imagine a father putting his daughter in such danger.

"Maybe it would have been easier if he hadn't, but what family roots I have are in that mansion. I still want to believe this talk of curses is all just superstitious nonsense. But to be safe, I took on the cleaning of the place myself. Even if there weren't a curse, I couldn't let strangers dig through my grandparents' stuff. I may not have known them well, but I owe their memory the dignity of a family member burying the family skeletons, so to speak."

"What was 'Anthony's grand obligation'?" Kendell asked.

"It was never explained in the journal. According to Dad, that lack of explanation was one of the telling messages that Anthony was half of a split personality. And of course, the two names, Anthony and Antoine, are practically the same. At first Dad thought he was just trying to hide from his past, and that might still be true. Anthony Laurette became well known for his building designs, which might be difficult for someone with a mental disorder. And if he really had lost his mind, he'd have ended up in one of the mental wards. I'm hoping to find more family diaries. There's six attics in the damn building plus countless hiding places. So far, I've only managed to clean out two of the storage spaces."

Myles knew what Kendell was going to say even before she set down her cup. "We'd be happy to help."

Samantha shook her head. "Thank you, but I'm not putting anyone else at risk. I promise, though, if I find anything pertinent to your pipe tool or the Malveaux family, I'll let you know."

11

"We need to get that tool back." Kendell didn't see any alternative as they walked along the levee, doing their best to avoid the groups of drunk tourists.

Myles had been suspiciously quiet after their meeting with Samantha. "That thing's dangerous. I'd be happy to leave it with the authorities."

"There are no authorities, not for situations like this. The police will rule Marilyn's death an accident. It's kind of the perfect crime when you think about it. With so many witnesses, trying to prove she was murdered would be insane."

He turned to lean against a railing and look out across the river. "The knife going into her throat wasn't the whole story, though. I doubt tires blow out on parade tractors for no reason. Those things must be checked out pretty thoroughly. I can accept the pipe tool killing Marilyn as part of the curse, but the tool didn't puncture the tire. That had to have been done deliberately."

His insight surprised her sometimes. "Add that to our run-in with the thugs at Float World, and I think we know where to start looking for our murderer. But again, the police aren't going to listen. Even if we could somehow prove the tire had been tampered with, there's no way to prove her stabbing herself wasn't an accident."

"Isn't that what detectives do—try to find the unlikely connections?"

Kendell's emotions were a jumbled mess. She couldn't forgive the man who'd stolen Cheesecake. He still needed to pay for the abduction, and involving the police might still put her dog in more trouble since she bit the thief. Then there was this strange connection she felt regarding the pipe tool. It was like she was responsible for something she had no control over. She'd just bought the damn thing, not performed the curse. But there was also an indefinable thrill when she thought about investigating a paranormal murder with Myles.

As she saw the situation, the bottom line was the question of where the pipe tool would end up. "If we solicit the police's help or not, we still have to go to the station. They have the pipe tool as part of their investigation. If they rule it an accident, what happens to the knife? We still have the receipt from the antique store. They'll vouch for us if the police need further assurance that it's ours. I've got too many questions to just walk away."

"So we just walk into the station and ask them to return

our blood-soaked knife? You don't think that's going to look suspicious?"

She tried to play out how events might transpire. Any questioning that delved too deeply into their history with the tool would get uncomfortable fast. "In all likelihood, they'll just laugh at us. I'll bet they've got a whole file of people walking in with tales of encountering dangerous ghosts or being cursed by voodoo priestesses. We'll endure a little humiliation. When they realize they've got no reason to keep the knife, we'll get it back. We have to at least try. And if they don't return it to us, we need to know it will be kept securely out of the public's hands."

THE LIGHT-GREEN WALLS and fluorescent lights gave Myles a mild headache. The institutional metal chair hurt his back. All that was missing was a pair of handcuffs to complete the experience of being questioned in the police station. "What are we doing here?"

A uniformed policeman stood near the door while another man in a business suit stood next to him—clearly also a cop, based on his stance. The detective across the table produced the pipe tool from his pocket. "We have a few questions. How long have you each lived in New Orleans?"

Myles couldn't imagine why that would matter. "Seven years. I came down for college and decided to stay after graduation."

Kendell kept her eyes down, making her look guilty. "I

was born here. But I've spent most of my life in California. I only returned to attend college."

The detective made a note on his pad. "Do you have family here?"

"Only my father. My parents are divorced."

"No siblings?" The detective's questions were beginning to get on Myles's nerves.

"Just me." She didn't sound afraid, but something in her voice made Myles feel protective of her.

"What do you know about this pipe tool?" At least his questions were starting to sound less creepy.

"We bought it at a shop on Royal. It was stolen a few weeks ago."

He made some more notes on his pad. "And you didn't report the theft?"

"We only paid fifty dollars for it. Since we got my dog back, we didn't see any point in getting the police involved."

He set his pen down. "Your dog was taken too?"

"It's a long story. She swallowed the damn thing, so the thief took her. But we got her back once she shitted it out."

The man in the suit near the door rubbed his chin. "What kind of dog?"

Kendell smiled for the first time since they'd walked into the police station. "Lhasa apso."

He nodded slightly. "Makes sense. Dogs are intuitive anyway, but the closer they are to their wolf ancestors, the more in tune they are to people and things around them."

The detective at the table cleared his throat. "Can I continue?"

"Sorry, didn't mean to interrupt." But the man's tone

made it clear the detective was merely asking the questions. It was the man in the suit who was really in charge.

"We'll want an affidavit regarding the theft and recovery."

Myles couldn't sit silent any longer. "The death was an accident. There was a whole crowd of people who saw what happened. Why are we being questioned?"

The detective must have dealt with far more belligerent interrogations. "We're simply trying to understand what happened. You did come to us after all."

"Not to be put in a room and grilled like criminals. Do we need a lawyer?"

The man by the door removed his glasses and began cleaning them. "I think I can handle this, Detective. Thanks for your help."

The man across the table made a display of flipping his notepad closed as if he'd gotten to the bottom of something. "No problem, Lieutenant."

As the uniformed policeman and detective left the room, the lieutenant motioned to the one-way mirror to turn off the recording devices. "My name's Lieutenant Joe Cazenave. Anytime I talk to someone, I'm required to have an entrance interview for the police records. I'm afraid we do so many they start feeling a little overly formal. I apologize."

Kendell loosened up her shoulders and lifted her head. "Why don't you just ask us what you want to know?"

"There is the truth people accept to get through their daily lives, and there are ideas they only entertain when they feel they are among friends. A police station is hardly the kind of place that makes people feel at ease.

Nonetheless, I'd like to ask what you believe to be true about the death of Marilyn Fontenot. Not just the facts, but also what lies below that reality."

Myles stared into the lieutenant's eyes. Something about the old-fashioned glasses made them appear strangely translucent. He chalked up that impression to the reflection off the green-tile walls. "We've spent some time researching the pipe tool's history. It was originally a present to the baron Malveaux from his young daughter. The story we've uncovered suggests she committed suicide with the knife, but it's something of a mystery."

The lieutenant stared at Myles from behind the glasses for some time before nodding. "An old, mysterious death and now an unfortunate accident involving the same seemingly harmless weapon. Certain superstitious individuals might try and make a connection between the two."

Kendell grasped Myles's hand under the table. "We're both college educated. But since you asked us to be at ease with ideas that might not be accepted by the general population, what if the death was of supernatural origin?"

He sat in the chair vacated by the detective and picked up the pipe tool. "I have the unenviable task of being our department's investigator into the paranormal. As you can imagine, we get people walking in the door all the time with wild claims of being cursed or chased by a vampire. You wouldn't believe some of the stories. Being the police, we have to take them all seriously. Most of my fellow officers are well trained on how to handle ninety percent of what comes in the door. But that last ten percent, the ones that might have some merit beyond the explanation of one of the parties being blind drunk at the time, end up on my desk."

"You think this thing is cursed?" Kendell asked.

"I didn't say that. I only told you about my job specialty so you'll understand why I ask some of my questions. I'd like to start off with you telling me your history with this item."

Myles felt certain Kendell was about to spout off about his ability to read past energy. To prevent being sent to the loony asylum, he recounted their history with the pipe tool while leaving out any mention of their experiment into what he could do. The history lesson from the jeweler had the lieutenant feverishly jotting down notes. To Myles's surprise, however, he showed only minimal interest in the events at Float World.

The lieutenant consulted his notes. "The Malveaux curse isn't one I've run across before. This could all be just another wild goose chase. Lord knows I've been on enough of them. Miss Summer, you might ask your father about any family history regarding the names Myles has given me. If there is some kind of paranormal activity, these items often search out descendants of the original parties. I wouldn't expect anything to come of it, though. If there is some connection, please let me know."

Myles had never been a big fan of the police, but certainly, a death demanded some investigation. "What about the tractor breakdown? You don't find that suspicious?"

"Have you ever known a Mardi Gras parade to run on

G.A. CHASE

time? Any city kid with a chauffeur's license thinks he's qualified to drive a tractor in a parade. Most of them don't even know how to properly stop one. Add in some dry-rotted tires and our streets' potholes, and you get a pretty good idea of why the processions are so slow. Give me a farm-raised field hand any day. At least they know how to handle one of those beasts. There simply aren't enough experienced tractor operators who are willing to deal with drunk tourists running out into the route, beads being thrown in their eyes, and maneuvering the long floats down our tight streets. Almost every Mardi Gras season, we get some parade accident caused by an inexperienced driver."

He put the pipe tool in a plastic evidence bag. Kendell pointed at what he was doing. "Will we get that back?"

The bag remained unsealed. "Even with your story, there's no indication of wrongdoing. If you don't want to make a formal request for an investigation, there's only so much I can do. The department is more than happy to mark cases like this as merely accidents. So technically, I can't hold this for evidence. But if there is some—well let's just use the word—*curse* associated with it, I can keep it from causing any harm. It is private property, though. So if you ask for it back, I will have to give it to you."

Myles thought they were better off without it, but Kendell clearly had other ideas. "I think I'd like to keep what's mine."

Before the lieutenant passed the tool across the table, he drew a symbol on the back of his business card and signed the bottom. "Should you decide this thing is better off

126

secured from causing harm, take it to the abandoned World Trade Center building and hand the guard my card."

Myles wasn't ready to let the opportunity to talk with someone who'd been involved with the paranormal slip by. "From your investigations, have you ever run across truly cursed items? Do you believe in them?"

The man tapped his pencil against the table as he considered his answer. "I've noticed that bad luck follows some people and objects. But for there to be a victim in a crime, there also has to be a perpetrator. Things don't act on their own. In the case of your pipe tool, there would have to be a murderer to have used the object. Marilyn Fontenot was a busybody reporter. I'm not saying she didn't have enemies, but they aren't the kind of people to cause physical harm. The high-society types are too self-absorbed for such behavior. Find me someone who really had it in for Miss Fontenot, and I'll take your claims more seriously."

"I wasn't pushing for an investigation. I was just hoping for some clarification on what you thought was real."

"Mr. Garrison, I do my best to be open-minded on the subject of reality. But I seldom find that trait in those around me. I find if I view every idea I have with skepticism people are more willing to listen."

BACK OUT ON THE STREET, Myles tried to come to grips with what Kendell had done. "Why on earth didn't you just leave that damn thing with the police? I know we didn't want to request an inquiry because of Cheesecake's involvement.

But he might have given our story at least some investigation even if he wouldn't admit it to us."

"Don't you get it? He was afraid of the pipe tool. It really is cursed. He just didn't want to admit it."

The late afternoon lit up the sky in shades of oranges, pinks, and reds. The colors reminded him of the bloodshot eyes of the Mardi Gras revelers sobering up from the afternoon's activities only to dive back into the evening's debauchery. "It's dangerous, Kendell. I don't want you to get hurt. And we both know I can't keep that thing with me. Whoever took it the first time may come back for it."

He knew she was holding the tool in her pocket. "That's another thing. Someone clearly thinks of this as a weapon. I appreciate Lieutenant Cazenave's position as paranormal investigator, but I suspect he's something of the laughingstock of the department. If we're going to really get him on our side, we'll need more evidence."

Women were a constant mystery, but even he knew when one was hiding something important. "What aren't you telling me?"

The streets were filling up with the evening dining crowd. She motioned him toward a secluded corner of Jackson Square near the wrought-iron fence and under the trees. "I asked my father about the names we've run across, specifically Malveaux since that's what started this whole adventure. I'd never seen him blanch like that before. He's from the Boston area. He said when they were courting Mom used to tell tales that had been passed down through her family. Her maiden name was Broussard."

They had run into many names since they found the

pipe tool, but Broussard wasn't one he remembered. "Did she know the name Malveaux?"

"I don't know. Dad wouldn't tell me anything, only that I shouldn't mention that name around her. Ever. The way he said it sent a shiver up my back like he was yelling the warning at me. He wasn't, but I knew inside what he was saying was important."

Myles had dated women from all across the country. The lure of attending college in New Orleans had a way of attracting any graduating senior who could con their parents into believing it was more about the education than the nightlife. "I never would have suspected you were a native."

"I'm not. At least, I don't feel like I am. Mom comes from one of the old New Orleans families, but you wouldn't know it. My parents met down here in college. They divorced when I was still in elementary school." She looked up into the ancient live oak. "I don't think I was even consulted as to where I'd grow up. They simply decided I'd stay with Mom. She used to say getting divorced was like having an anchor chain cut off her. She wasn't referring to Dad but to New Orleans. She took the opportunity to move us out to California, which honestly suited her better than here, but I was always close to Dad. So when I graduated from high school, he invited me down here to check out the colleges."

"And during those years growing up, your mother never talked about her past?"

Kendell's shrug lifted the shoulders of her jacket. "I never wanted to hear about it. California was my home.

New Orleans sounded so old-fashioned. She never impressed me as the Southern-belle type. I think she was just happy to leave her past behind. Dad used to tell stories of his time down here—typical frat-boy stuff. Mom would just roll her eyes once he started recounting some adventure."

"All the more reason to get rid of this thing. If your family is involved—"

She broke in. "I don't feel in danger, though. If it is a curse, it's not aimed at me. I have to know what my role is in this mystery. You're the one who can read energy, but I swear there's something about this pipe tool that makes me not want to let it go."

Myles remembered his feelings of protection regarding Serephine while he experienced her unintended suicide. "Like you're trying to prevent it from harming someone else? But wouldn't that be just as easily done by giving it to the police?"

"It's more than that. I don't have words for the feeling. All I know is I won't be able to rest until I know my connection."

"All right, Nancy Drew. What's our next step?" he asked.

As she scanned the buskers and artists outside the iron fence, he knew what she was going to say before she said it. "I want to go back to Professor Yates. If I hold the tool and he uses that weird contraption on me, maybe he'll be able to tell me something useful. He did say he thought the pipe tool would find its way back to us and that we should bring it to him once it was returned."

---

12

*M*yles didn't know what to expect as he and Kendell wandered along the run-down warehouses that covered the wharf. He knew the Bywater neighborhood that was a short walk from the French Quarter well enough. Friends of his in the service industry found rents in the eclectic area more reasonable than those close to the action. But the once-industrial area of the Bywater that bordered the river wasn't a place he'd frequented. The wood of the old piers squished under his feet. The pilings rumbled as a freight train edged along the tracks, blocking off their access to the neighborhood.

"This must be it." Kendell pointed to a newly painted red door in what otherwise looked like an abandoned office.

The boarded-up windows, rusting corrugated metal walls, and rotting roof beams left him with the impression that Professor Yates probably didn't pay much rent, if any. The place looked more appropriate for squatters or drug users than someone seriously investigating the paranormal. "Are you sure you want to do this? I know he said he could help, but right now, I'm thinking we're being conned."

"He hasn't asked us for money. What's the harm in finding out if he does know something? We haven't exactly run across a lot of people who have offered to help."

Myles hit the door buzzer. "True, but he still reminds me of a snake-oil salesman."

Professor Yates opened the door and rubbed his eyes like he'd just gotten up from a nap. The old man wore tatty jeans and a new white T-shirt that still had the creases, indicating he'd just pulled it from the package. With his gray hair tied back in a short ponytail, he at least appeared less of a charlatan than he had while working his trade as a mystic around Jackson Square. "Did you bring the pipe tool?"

Of course. Why else do you think we're here? But Myles repressed his cynicism. "We were able to get it back from the police. There's a new death associated with it."

The professor widened his eyes and perked up on hearing the news. "Let's have a look."

Kendell searched her leather satchel and pulled out the tool. But instead of handing it over, she kept it clutched in her hand. "There's something else I'm curious about. The longer I'm around this thing, the more I believe I have a connection to it. I wish I could explain it better. The thing doesn't feel dangerous to me. A better description would be protective, but I don't know if I'm supposed to protect it or it's protecting me."

The professor motioned toward an office behind the empty receptionist's desk. "I have some equipment back here that might help me read your energy better. The mobile unit I use around the Quarter has its limitations."

To Myles, the word *equipment* seemed to overstate the pile of wires, metal boxes lined with dials, and oscilloscopes that cluttered the previous supervisor's desk. The professor whistled a tune Myles couldn't identify as he hooked Kendell up to what looked like an old lie detector. From the frayed wires, yellowed plastic, and missing nobs, the investigative tool could have been salvaged from a pile of junk. With her looking like she was in danger of being electrocuted, the professor proceeded to place the pipe tool under a bell jar that had similar sensors attached to the outside of the glass.

The old man took a seat at the desk. "I must ask you both to remain quiet while I adjust the settings. Different vocal vibrations mess up the energy a person projects."

Myles reminded himself to be open-minded. Kendell was right. There weren't a lot of people they could turn to for answers regarding the paranormal aspects of their investigations and even fewer who approached respectability. The professor appeared more serious without the steampunk outfit he'd worn the last time they saw him. He methodically adjusted one dial after another in silence, not resorting to the constant banter typical of every fortune-teller and sideshow hustler in front of Saint Louis Cathedral. It took the man nearly half an hour to get all of the different colored lines on the oscilloscope to line up.

Professor Yates sat in the large leather chair, staring an unreasonably long time at the lines that moved in unified waves across the screen. *He's either stoned, fallen asleep with his eyes open, or lost in a trance.* But again Myles kept his mouth closed. Throughout the experiment, Kendell did a remarkable imitation of a statue.

Finally, the old man sat forward and scribbled a name and address on a scrap of paper. "Meet me here tonight at nine."

Myles couldn't take it any longer. "You have to be fucking kidding. After all this time and the magic show, all you have to tell us is 'meet me here at nine'? We deserve more than that. You must have seen something on that stupid readout."

The professor lifted the bell jar and pulled out the pipe tool as Kendell removed the sensors from her head and hands. "For the last two decades, I've devoted my time to researching human energy. I stay in New Orleans because some of the oldest studies, dating back hundreds of years, are still being conducted here. In many ways, I'm still a student. If a doctor sees something he finds mysterious on a patient's test, he calls for a second opinion. That's all I'm doing."

Kendell put the last of the wires on the desk. "So you did see something."

Professor Yates pointed his glasses at the now quiet oscilloscope. "The lines aren't supposed to mesh up like that. People have unique energy patterns. Once I learned how to identify them, it wasn't too difficult to build my little mobile unit to read people in general terms. Physical objects also have an energy readout. Atoms are constantly in motion, so everything is really only made up of energy. But animals and inanimate objects exist on very different wavelengths, as I'm sure you can imagine. Once I adjusted for your biological rhythms and that tool's metallic signature, I was left with two energy patterns that perfectly lined up. That's not supposed to happen. I've seen all kinds of readouts using this thing on people with their objects. Everything from intersecting lines that look like they're doing battle with each other to random oscillations that never touch. I'll be honest. I have no idea what it means when they perfectly match. But I might know someone who does. Tonight. Nine p.m. She doesn't like to be kept waiting."

~

"I KNOW THIS PLACE." Myles didn't like frequenting the area above Bourbon Street after dark and even less so with Kendell at his side. Many of the houses had been remodeled by people not familiar with the area, but full gentrification was still millions of dollars in the future for that handful of city blocks. The places where drug dealers conducted their illicit trade would soon be luxury condos. For the moment, though, it still wasn't a place to venture into unarmed.

She shivered slightly beside him. "It's a perfumery. How would you have heard of it?"

The mostly bare-wood exterior couldn't have been painted in decades. Only the yellow glow from the windows indicated there was any activity in what otherwise looked like an abandoned building. The faded sign out front, Scratch and Sniff Perfumery, was so weather-beaten it could have easily been from a previous era. "Strippers frequently stop by the bar after work. They've mentioned this place. It's one of the few establishments that will make perfumes the performers can use inside their G-strings. I think she calls her product Sensual Scents for the Sensitive Stripper."

"Fancy." Kendell's diminished tone and judgmental glare indicated she wasn't impressed.

"Hey, it wasn't my idea to bring you here. I still think Professor Yates is a quack."

"Maybe he is, but whatever he saw on his equipment made me think he wasn't trying to con us. If he was after our money, he would have come up with a more elaborate explanation of his results, and I doubt he'd bring in someone else for a piece of the action. Let's see where this evening takes us." She headed up the crumbling brick steps toward the rough-hewn wooden door.

Myles followed her, feeling a little like Hansel to her Gretel, stupidly entering the witch's lair. He breathed just a little easier when Professor Yates, who was still in his jeans and T-shirt, opened the door. At least they had the right place and didn't have to make their own introductions. "Right on time. Madam de Galpion is in the back. Don't let this establishment fool you. Mixing up fragrance potions is only her way of making a living. She's really quite skilled in the paranormal."

The shop appeared more like a chemistry lab than a retail establishment. Glass-fronted cabinets lined the walls filled with small brown jars. Their neatly typed labels and commercial logos made it clear these weren't homemade concoctions. A large industrial refrigerator stood against the back wall. A woman's soft voice of welcome sounded more like a song than spoken words. "Bring them back, Cornelius. I'm ready."

Myles had encountered enough people of creole descent to recognize Madam de Galpion's look—chocolate-brown skin, penetrating black eyes, and an aura of the mystical. But unlike the women who made the most of their ancestry by wearing robes and headscarves, Madam de Galpion was dressed as a professional businesswoman in a tailored silk blouse and conservative brown skirt.

The woman's office didn't appear big enough for three guests, so Myles remained in the doorway as Kendell took a seat opposite the striking woman. Chemical stains intermixed with irregularly shaped burn marks covered the table between the two women.

She reached out across the work desk. "Give me your hands, *ma chère*."

"We have some questions." Myles was getting a bit tired of people telling him and Kendell what to do without offering any explanations.

The woman's eyes were so dark he couldn't differentiate the pupils from the irises. "I won't be answering them."

Kendell took the woman's hands and turned to Myles. "It's okay. Let's just let her do her thing."

Madam de Galpion took one of Kendell's hands and rubbed it between her own. She then lifted it to her nose and took a deep breath. The ritual was repeated three more times before she spoke again in her smoky lounge-singer voice. "Let me see the pipe tool."

Kendell pulled the golden cylinder from her coat pocket

and set it on the desk. The woman barely looked at it. She pulled a small brown-glass jar from a drawer of the desk, drew some liquid from it with an eyedropper, and applied three drops to the tool. Then, as with Kendell's hand, she rubbed the tool between her hands and sniffed at the results.

"Can you at least tell us what you're doing?" As near as Myles could tell, the whole show should have been put on in Jackson Square where the tourists could chip in some money. The woman had a remarkable way of building emotional tension.

She placed the pipe tool into a burn depression on the table and rubbed her fingers together. "Smell is the least studied of our senses. Eyesight can be measured and compensated for with glasses or augmented with magnifying lenses. The same can be said for hearing. Even taste is better understood than smell. And yet, for some people, a simple whiff of wildflowers can unlock their earliest childhood memories. No other sense has the power to reveal like smell."

"That's not really an answer." Myles didn't want to make the woman cross, but so far, neither she nor the professor had been very forthcoming.

She looked at him and frowned. "You are an impatient person, *mon cher*. I'm only just beginning my olfactory investigation. Like my friend Cornelius and his investigation on people's energy, I find odor can be a defining characteristic. The fragrances I create mix with a person's body chemistry to form a unique scent. My investigation tonight will help me identify how Miss

Summer and this odd little tool share a unique historical bond. Now if you don't mind, I have a number of tests to perform, and talking distracts my nose from its mission."

Myles stood silently in the doorframe as the small room filled with a cornucopia of fragrances. Just when he felt sure he was about to pass out from the overload of smells, Madam de Galpion activated a ventilation fan to cleanse the air. His relief lasted only until she began again with a new series of scents. By the end of the hour, his sinuses were burning from the odorous potions.

She lit an incense stick and placed it in a hole in the desk. Holding the pipe tool in her long slender fingers, she turned it above the rising veil of smoke. "Have you identified the inscription?"

Kendell relayed what they'd learned of the tool's history but stuck to the facts relayed by Mr. Boudreaux and the antique store, leaving out any mention of the deaths or suspected curse.

Madam de Galpion returned the pipe tool to Kendell. "This item is safe in your possession. The same is not true for all descendants of the Malveaux family. It's tasted of their blood recently. I'd recommend keeping it away from anyone of that lineage. You will know who they are."

"How will I know?"

The mysterious woman tapped her blouse. "You will feel their presence like a weight on your heart."

Kendell stared at the pipe tool. "What is my connection?"

"In a magnet, the positive is attracted to the negative. Energy moves between the two poles. No object or person is fully good or evil. We're all a mixture of both. Your being is the complement to the pipe tool's energy, *ma chère*. That is why Cornelius's equipment read the two of you as a smooth wave. From the scents I generated, I can confirm a shared past, but what that means, I cannot say."

Professor Yates, who had remained quietly in the corner for the entire procedure, spoke up. "It isn't for us to define your destinies. I wouldn't even presume to make a recommendation. But know that there is help available should you wish it. For now, that's the best we can offer."

Myles escorted Kendell out of the shop and into the cool night air. The sounds of Bourbon Street and the competing live bands that occupied every establishment beckoned them away from the mysterious and back toward the nightlife he knew so well. "Do you get the impression every person we meet knows more than they're saying?"

She snuggled close to his side. He suspected she was looking more for support than warmth. "I think they don't know. If I were to guess, I'd say Cornelius Yates and Madam de Galpion are busy comparing notes as we speak. Research takes time."

Though he knew she was right, being in the middle of a murder mystery didn't inspire patience.

13

The sight of Cheesecake basking on the sunlit wood floor warmed Kendell's heart. She hated rousing her dog from her favorite hangout. The only two things that always made her spring to her feet were the offering of a snack or the prospect of a walk. Even so, as Kendell connected the leather leash to the dog's collar, Cheesecake only lifted her head as if to ask, "Do we have to?"

Kendell jiggled the leash to shake her dog's tags. "Come on, girl. We're going to go have lunch with Myles."

Cheesecake stood and performed a couple of her dog imitations of yoga stretches. Kendell had never been much into yoga, but then, she'd yet to find a studio that catered to both dogs and their human companions. One final shake, and the elderly Lhasa was good to go.

Kendell smiled down at her dog as they walked along Decatur Street. She considered dogs to be universal ambassadors of goodwill, and Cheesecake was a credit to her species. Even the gruffest business owner would brighten and give a playful salutation on seeing the small, shaggy dog with attitude. Each greeting made the old dog walk with just a touch more swagger. This was her street. The gutter punks might take shelter in the entrances of closed establishments, but even their scraggly mutts acknowledged the regal grande dame. Not one of the young pups would be so impertinent as to yip or bark as she passed.

By the time Kendell and Cheesecake made it to the small outdoor café, the dog was back to her commanding self. On seeing Myles, she even gave a lurch of the leash to move Kendell along a bit faster.

Myles, like any intelligent man with good taste when it came to women and their dogs, gave Cheesecake a warm greeting and pat on the head before turning to Kendell. "How's your girl doing today?"

Kendell playfully ruffled the dog's ears. "She's doing better. Now that I'm convinced that pipe tool really is cursed, I've been more concerned about its effects on her. As bad as that night hunting down her abductors was, it would have been far worse if I'd known what she was experiencing. Swallowing a cursed item can't be healthy."

"From the noises she made, I'd guess the perpetrators were the ones most in danger."

Once they'd taken their seats, Cheesecake curled up against Kendell's leg. "Marching in the Krewe of Barkus helped, but it's been an exhausting two months for her. I still can't fall asleep until I've triple checked the doors and windows. It helps knowing you're only a tap of my phone away." She wanted to thank him again for all he'd done, but after the first dozen attempts, she realized the correct words just didn't exist.

"You're more than a friend, Kendell. And that goes for your dog too. Now what's our next move? Until we figure out who stole the tool from us in the first place and murdered Marilyn, neither one of us is going to get any peace. I assume you're still committed to conducting our own investigation without help."

She pulled out the pipe tool and laid it on the table as if it too should be a part of the conversation. "The police won't help. Lieutenant Cazenave seemed very reputable. He could have bullshitted us with some story about looking into our suspicion then put the tool in a box never to be seen again. Even if we do find evidence of wrongdoing, it'll have to be pretty convincing for him to risk further ridicule from his department. And though what Professor Yates and Madam de Galpion told us was comforting in a confirmation kind of way, I'm not sure I trust either of them when it comes to an actual investigation."

Myles gave the waitress their orders. He included an appetizer of cheese sticks for Cheesecake. "I just wanted to make sure you didn't have a change of heart. No one would blame you. So we need to figure out why Marilyn was murdered and who did it. I feel like we're a little short on suspects."

Kendell leaned back in the outdoor metal chair and sipped at her sweet iced tea. "Whoever's behind it knows more about the curse than we do. That's saying something as the only person who knew anything is Samantha. And I don't think she had anything to do with it or she wouldn't have been on the float. I wish we could get a look at that diary she mentioned. You don't suppose Anthony, or Antoine, kept writing after the war?"

"I'm not that up on my Civil War history. I seem to recall some documentary saying soldiers often kept journals, but I'm not sure about the general population."

She petted Cheesecake with her foot. "From what we know, Antoine Malveaux sounded like a sensitive young man who was close to his sister and held his father in contempt. To me, he sounds like the kind of person who would keep his thoughts and emotions to himself. We know he could write. Let's say there is another journal out there. Who might own it?"

"I'd guess a family member. If he did write about the family being cursed, it's not the kind of information his descendants would want to be made public. So I wouldn't think someone would have bought the diary like we did the pipe tool. They would have inherited it."

Kendell tried to keep her excitement in check. She felt the familiar rush she'd had in college when her brainstorming with other students started to gel into ideas. "Remember what Samantha said? The curse would be aimed at the direct legitimate descendants of the baron. From what we know, he only had the two children, and Serephine committed suicide. So Antoine and Anthony *have* to be the same person. And that would mean Marilyn's killer was someone from her family."

Myles picked up the tool and turned it in the afternoon

light. "After over a hundred and fifty years, it could still be a distant cousin, aunt, or uncle. And that person would be in as much danger from the tool as she was."

"So they hired someone to steal it and put it in with her costume. That's the guy we need to find. We know he works for Float World."

Myles broke off a piece of French bread and passed it down to Cheesecake. "Didn't Mr. Boudreaux say his son-in-law drove a limousine?"

"Yeah, so?"

"He'd need a chauffeur's license for that, wouldn't he—the kind for driving tractors during Mardi Gras?"

Kendell didn't want to jump to conclusions, but the pieces seemed to be lining up. "Mr. Boudreaux also said his son-in-law showed an unusual interest in the business receipts. From his description, I got the impression the guy might take whatever work he could find even if it wasn't legal."

"I'm not crazy about confronting the thug who stole your dog. That gun isn't something I'm going to forget anytime soon."

Kendell's eyes moistened at the memory. "You did a pretty amazing job of disarming him."

His blushing never failed to give her butterflies. "I'm not sure showing up with a Frisbee is the way to go, but I don't think he saw me. If I were to go to Float World during working hours and ask for him, his reactions might tell us a lot."

She knew the person who abducted Cheesecake would recognize her immediately. And she hadn't noticed anything that would be useful in identifying the thug. Myles was right—it made more sense for him to go alone. But that wasn't the way they worked. "I'm going with you. Don't even try to argue me out of it."

~

A KNOT FORMED in Myles's stomach at the idea of taking Kendell to Float World. He didn't really even want to go himself. But avoiding places that made him uncomfortable could become a bad habit. To follow that path would inevitably make him a recluse. The more he learned to read energy, the more he had to face his fears of being overwhelmed by everything around him. And though each danger they faced together instilled a greater need to protect her, he had to respect her desire to also face her demons.

He kept his hand around her waist as they walked through the warehouse. Even in the light of day with people present, the memories of that night kept him on edge.

"We're looking for one of your tractor drivers, Link Le Rouge."

The overweight guard who manned the small office at the back could easily have been the model for the leading sculpture on the Bacchus float. He put down his sandwich and picked up one of the walkie-talkies that lined the back wall. "Someone's looking for you." He then pointed toward the open back gate, which was so large a small airplane would fit through it. "He'll meet you out by the picnic tables."

Kendell kept close to his side as they exited the warehouse. "You still think he's just going to tell us everything he knows?"

"I'm counting on Mr. Boudreaux being a good judge of character. He might not respect his son-in-law, but nothing about what he said led me to believe Link was all that dangerous. He sounded more like an opportunist."

She lifted her shoulders and rubbed her arms. "Maybe so, but this place gives me the creeps. At least one of those two guys had a gun that night."

He had run through the events of Cheesecake's abduction so many times he thought he could recount every word, every action, and every fear. The person who broke into Kendell's apartment would have been the taller and thinner of the two men. He needed to be agile enough to sneak through the window and escape down the extendable metal ladder and strong enough to do so with a twenty-pound angry dog under his arm. He was also the one forced to pick up the dog poop. That left the second man as the one with the gun. But which of the two was Link?

The lumbering blue tractor shook the cement pad as the gangly operator in overalls drove it unnervingly close to the wooden benches. "Looking for me?" His eyes darted from Kendell to Myles.

Myles didn't see any reason to beat about the bush. "We know Mr. Boudreaux. And I can see by the way you just looked at Kendell that you recognize her. Before this gets ugly, we thought you might have something to say about what went on here a couple of months ago."

To his relief, Link jumped down from the tractor instead

of firing it back up for some demented chase through the busy warehouse. "I have to hand it to you. After a month, I thought you'd given up on finding me. The fact that it's you two and not the cops means there's some haggling to be done."

Myles breathed a little easier. "No one was hurt that night. We didn't see much need to include the police. We'd like to keep it that way. Mr. Boudreaux is a sweet old man. I'd hate for him to suffer the heartbreak of finding out his daughter married a thief. We're just looking for information. What's your connection to the Malveaux object?"

Link rested his sinewy forearms on the weathered table. "Being a limo driver doesn't pay very well. I pick up as many odd jobs as I can find, but Magdalena has expensive tastes. I suppose I should have known marrying a jeweler's daughter wouldn't make for a frugal lifestyle. In desperation, I turned to the dark side of the Internet. There are forums where people list items they want stolen. Usually, these people are just looking to have their possessions returned from an ex-lover after a nasty breakup. On the forum, they're expected to list the value of the piece so those of us taking the job will know what to expect. I keep to items below five hundred dollars so if I'm caught, it's just considered petty theft. As you can imagine, those gigs don't pay much."

Kendell hugged her jacket close. "Someone put out a request to have my apartment broken into and the pipe tool stolen?"

The man smelled of diesel, which made Myles slightly

nauseous. "No, this post had been up for a while. It was considered the holy grail of requests. The job offered to pay five thousand dollars for any object displaying a calligraphy *M* with skulls. The pieces weren't described, but they were all assured to be small and inexpensive enough to qualify as petty theft. Every burglar in New Orleans has been keeping an eye out for such a piece for months. I usually work alone. But with this much money at stake, and having little time to break into your apartment before word got out about the piece, I enlisted the help of a friend. You don't have to worry about him. I'm the brains. He was just the muscle."

Myles's opinion of the man wasn't improving. Mr. Boudreaux seemed like a nice old man who was being used. "And you just happened to know that your father-in-law's forefather had made those items?"

"They came from Henri's shop? That's news to me. I keep an eye on the old man because people often bring in antique jewelry in need of repairs. Henri is one of the few artisans willing to take on such work. He also appraises a lot of stuff. If a person is so vindictive they keep a former lover's jewelry out of spite, they often end up wondering what it's worth."

Myles could see how such a contact would be useful for a petty thief, but that didn't explain Link's interest in the jeweler's search through the old receipts. "If you didn't know that the Malveaux items came from your father-in-law's shop, why were you so curious about his activities?"

"The old fool drew the *M* on the piece of paper with your address, didn't he? I knew I was onto something the instant I saw the scribble. I couldn't believe my good luck. The holy grail just fell into my lap."

Kendell put her hand on Myles's leg under the picnic bench. Not that he needed the warning. The last thing she'd want was to relive this man's kidnapping of her dog. "Once you had the pipe tool, why did you put it in with the Mardi Gras outfit?"

The man sneered in condescension. "You don't know much about crime, do you? The person commissioning the job never wants to meet in person. There's always some drop location or a middleman who doesn't know what's going on. I figured putting the tool in with the costume was just a means of transfer. When I heard about the accident, I could have screamed. I thought for sure that meant I'd never see a cent of that five grand. Boy, was I surprised when a bag of hundred-dollar bills showed up in my locker here at work. And it wasn't just the five Gs. They threw in an additional thousand. Six grand—that's a lot of driving drunk assholes around the tight streets of the Quarter in that damn stretch limo."

"You must have guessed it wasn't an accident," Kendell said.

"Lady, I don't get paid to think. If my patron wanted to tip me twenty percent, I'm not going to ask questions. Not that there was anyone to ask. I figured they wanted their generosity to be understood. Those of us on the forum rate a successful transaction. You can bet anyone who's heard the story is scouring every old jewelry box they can find, looking for that *M*. Now that we've had an example of what it looks like, I'd imagine a few are even buying engraving tools."

Kendell shook her head. "I'm confused about something. If a person was willing to spend that much money on the pipe tool that isn't worth very much, why not just offer to buy it? Seems like that would have been a hell of a lot simpler and cheaper."

"You two really are quite the pair. If a post shows up on the forum, we all know secrecy is important. Whoever wants an object stolen doesn't want people to know when they *have* the item."

Nothing the young thug said improved Myles's impression of him, but at least he didn't sound dangerous. "What about the tractor tire? The police believe it was just worn out."

"Never go into crime, okay? You'd suck at it. The contract I accepted was to steal the item and leave it with the parade costumes. If I'd gotten paid to sabotage the float, I'd end up knowing too much about the accident. As far as I'm concerned, knowing what I know, it was just an unfortunate incident and nothing else. You can go looking for the person who performed the tractor's maintenance, but like me, you're probably not going to learn much about who hired them. Hell, I can come up with half a dozen ways an old tire could end up on a work tractor. Now, if I've answered your questions, I really need to get back to work."

Myles didn't expect to see the two-bit thief again, but he saw no harm in reinforcing the point. "We don't mean you any trouble, but we do know who you are, where you work, and your father-in-law. We also know about the theft. Not that I suspect the police would care about a fifty-dollar item. I would hope you're smart enough to leave us alone."

Link stood and smoothed out his overalls. "If I never see you or that demonic dog again for the rest of my life, that'd be just fine with me."

Kendell quickly pulled out the notepad she always had with her. "Just one last thing. I'd like to have the web address of that thieves' forum. I promise I won't interfere with your business."

Link stared at her for a moment then pulled out a scrap of paper of his own. "It doesn't work that way. Someone from the forum has to vouch for you. But I've put you through a lot, and for that I'm sorry. I owe you. Give me your email, and I'll set you up. Just be careful what you say over there, and don't go giving out personal information if you know what's good for you."

Kendell was strangely quiet as they left Float World. At first, Myles thought she was trying to see their next move, but such topics she usually processed out loud. "What's up with you? I thought you'd be happy knowing that guy won't be lurking around your apartment. You and Cheesecake can sleep a little easier."

"It's not that. I am relieved to know Link was the abductor and I won't have to worry about him any longer. My mother is coming to town."

She seldom spoke about her family. He didn't want to overstep their friendship. "Are you going to ask her about your family's genealogy?"

She looked out across the river. "In spite of what Dad said about not bringing up the name Malveaux, I think I have to. I'm haunted by what the professor and Madam de Galpion said—and didn't say. If I have a family connection to this cursed item, I think I want to know."

"Do you think she'll have any answers?"

Kendell stopped to watch a cruise ship leave port and make its way downriver toward the gulf. "Dad says she has a wandering spirit like a tumbleweed with no roots. Even though they're divorced, they do still talk. I think that's why she's making a visit. He probably told her I'd been asking about my lineage. I know she doesn't like talking about her side of the family."

Myles seldom met his girlfriends' families, and Kendell wasn't even a romantic partner. Introducing him to her mother would imply that they might be more than just friends. "Do you want me to come with you?"

She turned to him and smiled. "Would it be too weird?"

"We're partners in this strange mystery. I don't know what kind of a relationship you have with her. My being there might make it harder for her to open up, or it might help you stay on track and ask your questions. I'll go if my presence helps, but I won't be offended if you think I shouldn't."

She thrust her hands deep into her coat pockets. "I should go alone. Maybe we can get together with her for dinner or something if she stays long enough. I do want you to meet her."

Kendell's blush reminded him that though the two of them were just friends, with all they'd been through, that term didn't cover their connection—*partners* would be closer. If he had trouble defining their relationship, he imagined she was just as confused. Women often liked second opinions when it came to their emotions.

14

*K*endell had never before bothered crossing the river to the small residential community that faced the French Quarter. Everything she wanted could be found a few blocks from her apartment. She never saw the appeal of a middle-class neighborhood with few restaurants and no shopping. The ferry crossing, however, provided a nice view of the Quarter. From out on the river, she used her phone to take a handful of snapshots of Saint Louis Cathedral. The hard pounding of the old steel boat against the wooden dock shook her back to her task.

As she exited the boat, she saw her mother standing at the top of the gangway. The woman had toned down her hippie attire from the last time they'd met. Even so, the flowing skirt, sandals, and billowy blouse looked too light for the cool spring afternoon. *At least she's not wearing tie-dye.* Their embrace was loving but short. "Aren't you freezing?"

Her mother pulled up the hem of her skirt to display colorful leggings. "Some of us don't live in peacoats, my darling daughter. You have such a lovely figure. I don't know why you insist on hiding it."

"I only bundle up when it's cold." But her mother had a point. The heavy garment needed a good dry cleaning after its extensive use over the last few months.

"I thought we'd get a coffee at a small café I know. But first maybe a private walk along the levee? Your father tells me you have some questions about my side of the family."

As they walked along the man-made berm to the bike path, Kendell marveled at the old homes. "I didn't realize this neighborhood was so historic. All I'd ever heard about the Westbank was that it was as close to suburbia as one could get and still be in New Orleans."

Her mother stopped in front of the old brick courthouse. "I had you meet me here for a reason. All this used to be our family's property."

She pointed down at a brass plaque embedded in the path. "Broussard Plantation 1802–1860." Kendell quickly read the historical description of the property. Other than the name and dates, she didn't see anything useful. "That was a long time ago."

"How much do you know about New Orleans before the War Between the States?"

"I seem to be learning more about it every day."

Her mother sat on a metal bench next to the path. "Sit with me while I try to untangle what I remember. I grew up in an amazingly boring family. At every big event, all the old folks would do is talk about the past. I swore if I ever had kids I'd never subject them to those hours of sitting around the dining room table listening to stories about dead people while the remains of the meal solidified on the fine china. My sister and I once calculated that every fifteen minutes of mind-numbing conversation resulted in half an hour of increased scrubbing to get the hardened food off the plates."

Kendell smiled at the thought of her bohemian mother and respectable aunt being young girls forced to sit at the family table and just listen without having anything to contribute. "Is that why you've never talked about our family history?"

Her mother wrapped an arm around Kendell's shoulder. "Maybe partly. My grandfather and granduncle used to get into arguments about what they'd heard growing up. As they were the oldest two members of the family, no one contradicted them or bothered to shut either of them up. Most of what I know is oral history. I'd really hoped to let the story die with me, but you have a right to know it if you want."

Kendell couldn't remember her mother ever opening that mental locker of her personal history. "I don't want to worry you, but I'm involved in an investigation. Dad said I shouldn't ask, but what do you know about the baron Archibald Baptiste Malveaux?"

Her mother let out a long, slow sigh. "Let me tell you about your ancestor first. The last one who owned land on this side of the river. Louis Broussard inherited the plantation from his father, who bought it after the slave trade moved across the river. Unfortunately, Louis was no farmer. Instead of focusing on what he could grow right here on this high ground, he wanted to develop the lowlands around the bend in the river. He was trying to develop a method of draining the bayou that covered most of the area downriver. But his experiments weren't cheap. Every year, he had to go across the river and borrow more money from the bank. And each year when he couldn't pay it back, he deeded more of this area to the banker."

"Don't tell me—the baron Malveaux?"

Her mother nodded. "This is where some grounding in antebellum history helps. During the war, the Yankee soldiers had a cruel practice when it came to the genteel ladies of the South. Any woman who insulted one of the curs was treated like a lady of the streets, a prostitute. What isn't written about in those history books, though, is the practice didn't arrive with the northerners. According to my grandfather and his brother, the baron Malveaux believed in diversifying his empire. Unsatisfied with simply making loans to developers, he built himself a series of brothels. In the days before the Storyville District, such establishments could be found in nearly every neighborhood. Blacks, Quadroons—whores who were one-quarter black but looked white—and even white prostitutes could be had if the customer had enough money. But the elite gentlemen of New Orleans, being wealthy and perverted, truly desired women of their own class."

Kendell looked out over the river, trying to envision her beloved city as being even more bawdy and less restricted. "Why would an upper-class woman allow herself to become a prostitute? I can see how it would happen during the war, but how did it happen before the war?"

Her mother hugged her close. "This is where the baron and our ancestor cross paths. By 1860, Louis had run out of useable land. This is also the point in the story where my grandfather and his brother had their most heated arguments. One believed Louis had been a complete fool for giving up the best land first, while the other argued he had no choice. Not that it mattered, then or now. The bottom line is the day came when Louis was out of options. He took the deed to the last remaining acres and headed to the bank to pay off his remaining debt. He'd be broke, but his plan was to pack up his family and leave New Orleans for good. No one knows what happened to him. But the next day, the baron showed up and forced Louis's wife and children— two girls and a boy—into indentured servitude. That was his little trick, you see. He'd get someone of breeding under his thumb then slowly whittle away at their savings until he could take their family in the socially acceptable version of slavery. The baron's upper-class gentlemen clients could then have the wives or children of adversaries as they pleased. Louis's wife and daughters were forced into prostitution, and his son was sent to work on the docks."

Kendell pulled her coat tight around her arms. "That's horrible."

Her mom removed her arm from around Kendell's shoulder and clasped her hands in her lap. "I wish I could tell you our story ends there. Not long after our ancestors found themselves beholden to the baron, he started having problems of his own. Not financial, unfortunately, but emotional. My grandfather didn't know the specifics, but apparently, the baron lost his family. There might have been a death—my family story was pretty vague. What was known, however, was that his wife left him and his son disappeared into the war. All the baron was left with was his riches."

Kendell tried to remember what she'd read about him after the death of Serephine. "So he became a recluse?"

"Unfortunately for us, no. He lost himself to his whorehouses. My great-grandfather was the product of Lilianna Broussard—daughter of Louis—and the baron Malveaux. Because it was an illegitimate union, the name Broussard was kept for the child. But the family legend is very clear that the baron is part of our lineage."

Kendell found it hard to breathe. She knew in her gut the story had to be true. For the cursed pipe tool to be safe in her possession, she would have to be descended from both the one who commissioned the curse and the one who had originally owned the piece. The baron's energy would have permeated the object. He'd kept it with him at all times. If just the curse energy was at play, she'd experience a desire similar to the tool's. She thought about her reactions to Samantha Laurette. As a direct descendent of the baron, that sweet woman would be in danger from the pipe tool. Kendell felt no such hatred. Inside her jacket, she squeezed the wretched metal cylinder, wishing she could crush the evil out of it. "And no one knows what happened to Louis? The family must have had some ideas."

"Just the speculation of old men. Some nights they would say he got drunk and the deed was stolen. Other tellings of the story had him falling off the ferry and drowning. I don't think anyone really knows."

Kendell looked past the restored houses to the empty military complex that bordered the neighborhood. She made a mental note to check the city's property records. If no one had claimed the property, she wasn't hopeful. With the confusion of land rights following the war, it was hard to know who property had really belonged to. "If it's just a silly old story, why do you avoid coming back?"

Her mother stared out across the river. "I wanted something different for my life than living with people I'd known since childhood. New Orleans looks like such a big city, but it isn't—not really. So many families here can trace their roots back hundreds of years that family trees end up looking more like twisted, intermingled wisteria vines. Cousins, second cousins, distant cousins, aunts, granduncles —you can't imagine how boring it all becomes. I once dated a boy in high school only to find out we used to play naked together as children in his grandparents' yard. His mother showed me pictures. The relationship didn't last long after that revelation."

In spite of the distance in their relationship, it never took long for Kendell to feel the bond with her mother. "I've been working with someone. We're not dating, but I think we're more than friends. He helped me out of a tough situation."

"Do you love him?"

With anyone else, even her father, Kendell would have laughed off the question, but her mother had a way of seeing past the trappings of everyday life. "He's not like the guys I usually date. I haven't seen a single tattoo on him. He can't carry a tune for shit. Watching him dance is kind of like watching a cross between the Paralympics and interpretive dance. His wardrobe is practically conservative."

"What does Cheesecake think?"

As a young girl, Kendell hadn't made any secret of her trust in her dog's instincts, even if her parents thought she was just projecting her impressions onto the animal. "She trusts him more than any boy she's met."

"That's saying a lot. Your father fell in love with me for my free spirit, but in the end, I failed his trust. There was never any infidelity. I simply couldn't be there for him like he needed."

Kendell felt the cell phone in her pocket. One press of a button, and Myles would drop everything to be at her side. Maybe he wasn't the exciting rebel looking to challenge the status quo or the musician who always understood her passion, but he gave her a feeling of safety she'd never known, not even as a little girl. "I'd like you to meet him."

15

*M*yles rubbed his temples. "Wait a minute. You now not only believe this thing is cursed, but you also believe you're descended from the baron who owned the pipe tool?"

Kendell had been pacing her apartment for the entire time it had taken for her to recount her afternoon with her mother. "That's not all of it. I think Louis Broussard is the one who commissioned the curse."

"You know I'm on your side, but you have to see how crazy that sounds." He got off the couch to take her by her shoulders. All her pacing was making him dizzy. He hoped the physical contact might settle her down. "We still don't have anybody other than us saying anything about a curse. There is something strange about the pipe tool. I'll give you that. But if there was a voodoo priestess performing curses —even if that was something that was only real in the past— don't you think someone would have mentioned it?

Professor Yates or that strange Madam de Galpion—hell, even Lieutenant Cazenave would have at least hinted that such things were real. Each time one of them gets close to saying something about that topic, it's in a dismissive tone. You are an educated woman. Doesn't that mind of yours rebel against the idea of superstitious nonsense?"

He'd hurt her. He could see it in her eyes, which started to glisten. "I thought you believed in me."

"Of the two of us, you're the intellectual. I'm the skeptic. Me being on your side doesn't change. Ever. All I'm saying is, convince me."

"Did I ever ask you to prove you saw that airplane? Or question your story about Serephine's suicide?"

She had a point, and it made his heart hurt. All she'd ever done was try to help him find proof of his ability. Never once had she questioned what even he wondered about himself. "I'm sorry. You're just always so good at providing the facts to back up any idea."

One of the characteristics he admired most about her was her ability to listen to reason even while being emotional. Most women he'd known needed a considerable period of time to cool off after they'd been provoked. "I suppose until we find a true witch or voodoo priestess, we won't know anything about curses for certain. But you did say you felt something strange about the pipe tool beyond Serephine's suicide. I know there were plenty of people who witnessed Marilyn's death, but we never bothered to have you read the tool. Having you see a recent death might prove useful. So far, every event you've experienced has been far in the past."

He hadn't given the idea of reading the woman's energy much thought. The events were well enough known. "I suppose it couldn't do any harm. At the very least, I'll be able to get some feeling of a recent death compared to one that happened long ago. Since it's the same object, me reading it like before could be a scientifically useful experiment."

She took his hand. Her soft voice made him think she was resigning herself to the obviously valid procedure. "We should do it exactly like last time."

"But you want to try something different?"

She kept her head down and looked up through her long eyelashes. "You're getting to know me a little too well. I was wondering if you could read me and the tool at the same time, kind of like how Professor Yates conducted his test."

"That's not going to tell us much about how Marilyn died."

"Fuck Marilyn. You asked me to prove the curse is real."

Her vulgarity made him smile. "We'll need a place where we can lie down next to each other."

"My bed's big enough. Unless that would make you too comfortable and you'd fall asleep."

He looked over at Cheesecake, who appeared less interested in the conversation than in finding the perfect position for lounging in the sun. "She won't mind?"

"Don't be silly. You came to her rescue. A girl doesn't forget things like that. She trusts you every bit as much as I do."

He wasn't sure being considered safe was completely a good thing. Gaining a woman's trust while steering clear of

G.A. CHASE

the dreaded friend zone was a complex game. "I've never tried to access this level of awareness while touching someone. The most likely outcome is I won't get anything from the tool."

Kendell kicked off her shoes and crawled onto the bed. "I know. I just want to see what might happen. You should lie opposite me with your feet near my head. That way we can hold left hands. It might feel more natural to you than trying to flip your hand over to hold mine or have my wrist across yours."

He reached down and yanked off his tennis shoes. "Why left hands?"

"That's not your dominant hand. I thought you might find it less distracting."

Lying on the large bed in the awkward position made him feel like a little kid. He let his hands fall naturally to his sides. "I should warn you: the first time I read an object's energy, I was a little kid, but I still remember the experience. I was terrified I wouldn't be able to find my way back to my mind and body."

She placed the pipe tool in his palm then put her hand in his. "So it's like an out-of-body experience?"

"I'd say it was more than that. 'Out of body' implies you're still in touch with your thoughts. What I experience would be closer to being someone else. Have you ever woken from a dream that was so intense you had to take a moment to remember who you were? It's kind of like that."

She squeezed his hand, pressing the pipe tool into his palm. "But you're not asleep."

"No, and that makes it more terrifying. I leave little

mental clues as I'm getting further into the experience. Like leaving a mental trail of popcorn so I can find my way home. I associate small memories with each level of consciousness. As I relax and nearly fall asleep, I remember the bed I slept on the first time I tried to read energy. It was a small twin bed with a cowboy blanket. I mentally feel the fuzzy fabric, hear the springs when I move, stuff like that. It's just a quick impression to help me remember who I am."

She wiggled her toes next to his head. The movement reminded him of how she often moved her fingers while she considered some idea. "Do you think I should have similar road markers?"

"In all likelihood, nothing's going to happen. But if you get scared, remember holding Cheesecake in your arms the first time you met. That memory should work as a mental rope to get you back to your life. Now if you're ready, just lie still, and try not to fall all the way asleep."

Myles began the familiar mantra that helped separate his mind from his body. *I am who I am.* Though he acknowledged the odd phrase sounded more like grounding himself in his life, the way he interpreted the words helped him let go of anything that wasn't *him*. By the time he'd let go of his body and even his name, he could turn his attention to the object he touched.

But he wasn't just touching a thing this time.

KENDELL STRUGGLED to keep her excitement in check. There was no one she trusted more than Myles. He'd done so much, but even more important was his belief in her. And now he was allowing her to share in his most intimate journey. They'd talked enough for her to know he seldom mentioned the ability with anyone, including girlfriends. For him to even attempt a shared connection made her heart flutter.

His touch calmed her thoughts like snuggling up in a warm blanket against the cool air of reality. She remembered a sensory-depravation experience a past boyfriend had talked her into once. As with that experience, she allowed her thoughts to float free. With one last thought about Cheesecake basking in the warmth of the afternoon light in the living room, she let go of her grasp on all that she knew.

She was a young boy lying on his bed. The light from his window was interrupted by the shadows of a peach tree whose limbs swayed in a light breeze. The smell of freshly mown grass hung heavily in the air. It was his naptime, but he wasn't tired. His hands closed around the wool blanket. He was who he was, and that included not just the little body that he barely understood. She was also a part of him.

Then, like a plastic bag filled with water and floating in the ocean, she and the boy, who were one and the same, emptied into the vast human experience.

In spite of feeling like she was a being made of water submerged in the ocean, Kendell struggled to breathe. Her body shook as she tried to surface for air. *Cheesecake!* She felt the soft puppy fur against her face. The small dog squirmed around in her arms to lick her chin. The little girl of long ago quickly gave way to the woman.

Kendell let go of Myles's hand and sat up on the bed. Sweat covered her forehead. Lazily, Myles opened his eyes. "You're okay. Focus on your breathing for a moment. Don't try to fight your thoughts."

"What the hell happened?"

He sat up to face her. "You had a little freak-out. Nothing to worry about. I used to get them all the time as a kid. Letting go of yourself is a little like staring into a spinning vortex. It makes you a dizzy and confused. The natural instinct is to fight your way back to what you know."

As she stared into his eyes, she saw the little boy she remembered. "How old were you?"

"When I first started this journey? I don't know, maybe five or six. I was young enough that school hadn't driven out the idea of magic. Before they're taught about reality, kids know a lot more than we give them credit for. Ever watch a child the first time they're given a balloon? It's like their whole life—which is only a couple of years—they've known that things fall when they're dropped. Then there's this ball that somehow is able to fly away. Magic. I think because I hadn't yet been filled up with grounding education as my known reality, it was easier for me to float away. I did warn you it could be frightening the first few times."

She pulled her knees to her chin. "How did you not lose your mind? I'm twenty-four, and that fucking freaked me out. I was pure consciousness without borders immersed in every other human soul. At least I'm old enough to have the words to describe it."

He lifted the pipe tool. "That's why we have something

to focus on. To read its energy, I first have to let go of everything that's *me*. But we don't exist in a void. People are all around us. They just don't realize that they too are little more than pure energy."

"I think you're onto something a lot bigger than psychometry."

He lay back on the bed. "We all have our specialties. Ready to try again?"

As she resumed her position, she wondered if she should have told him about being a part of him as a young boy. She could still feel his fear from so long ago. It would be so easy to love that kid and even more so the man he'd become.

~

MYLES once again held Kendell's hand. "It's okay to bail out anytime you want. I'll be right here beside you even when we are only pure energy."

She squeezed his hand as if she were giving him a hug. "I know. You're always there."

He did what he could to remain aware of her as they descended the levels of consciousness. Her presence was like a little pink ball of excited, innocent energy. As he rounded the road marker of himself as a young boy, his being merged with hers. The pipe tool that was to be their shared connection so closely matched her energy that he had trouble identifying which impressions were from the tool and which were from Kendell. His feeling of emotional upheaval wasn't unusual, but this was like being flung into a hurricane. Their hands squeezed. He couldn't tell which of them was performing the action.

Their connection was strong. Like battling quicksand by struggling, fighting the forces that surrounded them would only drag them further into the chaos. He forced calm into their union. The goal was to hear what the pipe tool had to say.

An intense hatred filled its soul. The blackness that infected it was even darker and grungier than the tobacco tar that it scraped off the pipe walls. It was like some slave meant only to clean the remains of other's vices. It couldn't take the energy any longer, but there was nothing it could do, no movement it could claim as its own. The experience of slavery was complete.

A strong jolt pulled it from the ugly wooden cylinder. This was its one shot. With its blade still extended, it aimed its weapon into the pulsing neck artery. The gushing blood bathed it in relief. It was at peace once again, fulfilling its true destiny.

Time had a very different meaning for the object than it would for a human. Like the hands of a clock spun backward, a force was driving it into hidden depths. Though the dichotomy of male and female didn't apply, the force was more directed than any previous attempt at the experience. And that force was like being led by the hand of a sweet, innocent child. The twister of emotions spun down to a calm day. But it wasn't the pipe tool he'd entered.

The sound of a woman's much-loved voice rang out across the field of wildflowers. "Delly, it's time for lunch."

"Coming, Grammy." The girl's small hands tucked the

figure she'd made of sticks under a blanket of leaves. A dandelion served as a pillow. "Just rest here. I'll be back after I eat."

The grass felt wonderful on her bare feet as she ran toward the picnic table under the live oak. Her family was already seated. Grammy had made sure there was a spot next to her for her favorite granddaughter.

She knelt on the wooden bench so she could reach her plate of fried catfish and grits. Her grammy always knew exactly what to make.

On the other side of the table, the old men were conducting their endless argument about the family's history. *Who cares?* But she'd been taught not to interrupt when the grownups were talking.

Grandpapa Alfred's frail body made her wonder how he managed such a booming voice. "You heard the story straight from Antoine just like I did. I just don't understand how you can be so dense."

Grandpapa Milton, though not her real great-grandfather, had a more genteel way of expressing himself. "He was an old man. Anyone would be pretty rattled in the head after serving in the War Between the States. Even the well educated believed in superstition back then. Just because he said all of his progeny would be cursed because of his father's evil doesn't make such nonsense real."

"And what of our father? You expect me to believe he just fell out of the pecan tree after spending his life in the orchards?"

Grandpapa Milton hadn't taken a bite out of the fried

chicken he waved like a stick to make his point. "You know as well as I we're not descended from Antoine."

"We come from the baron Malveaux. He's the one who was cursed. Had Serephine lived, she would have been every bit as at risk as her brother. Antoine was clear on that point. If those two were heirs to the curse, why wouldn't any of the baron's illegitimate children suffer the same fate?"

She liked Grandpapa Milton more than her real great-grandfather. He didn't yell as much. "Lilianna wasn't just another in his stable of whores."

Grammy put her hands over Kendell's young ears. Not that it mattered. She could still hear the conversation. It was just muffled. But she guessed it made Grammy feel better. "What have I told you two? Don't use words like that in front of Delly."

"Sorry. Of course you're right."

Grammy took her hands away and smiled down as Kendell took a big bite of the fried fish. No one could cook like Grammy.

Grandpapa Alfred smiled at his brother in the sickening way he did when he'd just beaten Kendell at checkers. "So you admit to the curse at last."

"I didn't say that. But purely for the sake of argument, if it were true, none of us around this table would be at risk. We both know who commissioned Madam Laveau, even if Antoine wasn't aware of our history."

She seldom saw Grandpapa Alfred go quiet. But when he answered, it was in a hushed, conspiratorial tone. "And that makes us guilty of any future misadventures that might befall anyone from the Laurette family? Am I really my brother's—or in this case, distant cousin's—keeper?"

"If we were only of Broussard blood uncontaminated by the evil Malveaux lineage, encountering one of the baron's personal possessions might bring forth the curse. But as we share the history of both the damned and the cursed, our people are the only ones who can stop the evil. At least that's what I got out of our conversation. It's been seventy years since our afternoon with that old coot. I've asked myself over and over why he bothered looking up all of his illegitimate half siblings if they, and us, weren't in danger. I think he was either hoping to find someone who could end the curse or recruit people to keep his descendants safe. It was like some grand obligation he'd committed his life to fulfilling. Now, if we could get our hands on the voodoo queen's diaries, we might finally know something."

The scene grew hazy. Quickly, the little girl took a bite of a butter roll to savor the last taste of her grammy's cooking from so long ago.

The whirlwind of emotional confusion returned. They were still joined together, but instead of returning to the surface of their lives, they sank deeper.

As the scene coalesced into a crisp vision of the pipe tool, he wondered if they'd returned to Kendell's bedroom. The tool, however, was not grasped between hands but nestled in the fine fabric of a silk pocket. Being an inanimate object didn't come naturally. An action in one form or another gave meaning to the experience. Simply rocking back and forth in the dark pocket aroused a fear that they might have to figure a way out without the benefit of some intensely emotional event.

Being a cylinder made of gold and steel did have a certain Zen-like quality. A feeling of belonging filled their consciousness. The tool had a purpose. It was a valued possession.

An energy wave overrode the experience of being useful. It was the beginning of the familiar black cloud that darkened every aspect of the tool. A hand reached into the pocket and threw it into a silver tray on a large oak desk.

Time had no reference without actions. How long the tool sat on the desk had as much meaning as how long a rock had lain by the ocean. A day or a thousand years— there truly was no difference.

A young girl's hand lifted the tool from its rest. From the first touch, the tool's blade yearned to taste the child's blood. The desire, any desire, was a new experience. There were still no thoughts that could be identified, but an overwhelming need to plunge its knife into the girl's soft flesh consumed every atom.

As the girl drew the sharp edge along her wrist, the dark energy separated the cells of her skin. Like a wheel spinning in sand, the thin blade sank deep into the warm vein, bathing it in the blood of fulfillment.

Myles felt his arm pulled nearly out of its socket by Kendell as she sat up. "I killed her. I killed them both. I felt my blade sink into both of them. I've never wanted to harm someone before, but that black hate overpowered me. There was nothing I could do to stop it. I didn't want to stop it.

I've never wanted anything more than to feel their blood all over me."

He took the pipe tool from their shared grasp and tossed it to the end table beside the bed. "Focus on your breathing. Let you, Kendell Summer, flow back into you. You are not a knife that just killed a woman and a little girl. The girl died long ago. Neither death was your fault. You are a woman living in New Orleans. Cheesecake is in the next room."

Kendell turned to him, panting. "Okay. I'm coming around. I am not a knife. I am not a knife."

He swung around on the bed and took her in his arms. "Give it a minute. Don't force your thoughts. Think about Cheesecake."

She put her arms around his. "I can't imagine how you survived that as a little boy. I saw him, you know—you as a little boy. I think I was him for a minute."

"I know. I should have expected you'd become a part of me, but it wasn't intentional."

Her tears wet his cheek. "Oh, God. You became a part of me too."

"Now, that I couldn't have foreseen. For what it's worth, I'm glad you got to see me as a little boy. And though you didn't invite me in, I'm honored to have had the experience of getting to know you better."

She pulled away to face him. "But I did invite you. I was the one who took us from Marilyn's death to my memory of that afternoon. You couldn't have known the way, and the pipe tool wasn't even there. I did that. I wanted you in me even more than that cursed tool wanted to be bathed in blood. But I still don't see how you survived taking that trip as a young boy."

"Well, I didn't try and enter an object back then. My early experiences of leaving my *self* behind were mostly no deeper than that ocean of consciousness you saw. I shouldn't have overloaded you on your first time out."

She snuggled back against him. "It wasn't your fault. I asked you to take me along. How did we get back to seeing Serephine's death?"

"I think that was your doing. Typically, I stay unfocused on these trips. That way, I can experience when the object has seen the most human energy. I think your spirit has a lot more direction than mine."

She put a hand to his heart. "I remember those picnics, but not that particular one. I never paid much attention to what my grandpapas argued about. Usually Grammy would play some game with me or ask me about the stick figures I made. She was the only one in my family who really understood me. I miss her something terrible at times."

He could still feel the warmth in his heart as she talked about the woman. "I've never inhabited someone who's still alive."

"I'm glad you were there."

MYLES WAS RELIEVED when they left the bed and returned to the living room. The only experience he could come up with that had been so intimate was sex, and that wasn't a comparison he wanted to make. She trusted him. They were partners. Danger still hung around them like the growing humidity of spring in New Orleans. This was not the time to introduce romantic notions into their relationship.

She brought a couple of beers from the kitchen. "Now are you convinced that the pipe tool is cursed?"

He'd forgotten that had been the whole point of their afternoon away from their bodies. "Your grandpapas sure sounded like they believed it, even Grandpapa Milton. I think he was just arguing it didn't exist so he wouldn't have to worry about every member of the family. And being the knife while it cut into Marilyn's neck and Serephine's wrist felt pretty convincing. Usually, I get the person's impression of the event, not the object's. I suspect that had to do with your unique connection to the tool."

"You used to talk about your experiences reading energy like you were reading a book. I get lost in a good book. Reading for me is like becoming one of the characters. But not like you and how you use psychometry. I think I understand what Madam de Galpion said about feeling a weight on my heart when I'm around someone under the curse. I have a duty to save them. That must have been what Anthony Laurette meant by his grand obligation."

Much as he wanted to hold her in his arms, they had work to do. "Then we'd better figure out who knows about this curse and stop them. I don't know if Marilyn's murder was an isolated crime or if there's more to come. But either way, we need to find the person responsible."

"Agreed. Do you remember Samantha talking about how her grandfather collected the genealogical record of the family? If we're right about this person learning about the

DOG DAYS OF VOODOO

curse from one of Antoine's diaries, and they are a part of the Laurette family who were originally the Malveaux family, we might be able to at least have a list of people to investigate."

The cold beer helped him return fully to the life he knew. "We should also check out what Marilyn was writing. I know Samantha said she just did fluff pieces, but if she was onto some family secret, she might have left notes. That could also be why she was killed."

"I hope you're right. One premeditated act of murder is a lot easier for me to deal with than some deranged individual out to kill off all of his relations. But I'll be keeping an eye on the dark-web forum just in case."

16

*W*here to keep the pipe tool continued to plague Kendell. Even though Cheesecake no longer displayed any unusual behavior, leaving the cursed item in the apartment when Kendell wasn't there left her in a continual state of worry. She removed her gloss-black electric guitar from its black alligator case and secured the tool in a pocket of the case's lining. At least having it on stage would alleviate the possibility of someone walking off with it unnoticed.

The Scratchy Dog was just beginning to fill with the usual Friday night customers. She performed better when the crowd started out small. Like the music itself, energy should build to a crescendo as the night progressed. Polly disagreed, but as the band's leader, she was always more concerned about the bottom line than the artistry.

From the first chord of "Born Under a Bad Sign," Kendell knew the night was going to be epic. Her fingers clawed at the strings like a cat ripping at its prey. The music she produced was raw and untamed. Her guitar absorbed her energy and screamed out for more. As the song ran out, her fingers instinctually moved to the opening riff of "Got My Mojo Working." She tried not to pluck the stings, but it was no use.

Polly would be pissed. The band's leader loved the crowd's adulation between each number. It let her shine. But that night, she'd just have to suck it up.

On stage, Minerva Wax was always a caged animal behind her drum kit. That woman could bash out a rhythm that spoke to Kendell's soul. Most nights, it was Minerva's hard-driving beat that carried the rest of the band. But not tonight.

Together with Scraper on bass, the rhythm section was the first to catch on to Kendell's energy. There would be no breaks between songs. This set would be one long, continuous driving force to be reckoned with by any who set foot in the club. Newcomers would have to get on the train or end up splat on the tracks.

By "Little Red Rooster," Lynn Seed had given up on her keyboards and joined Kendell, now in full Olympia Stain persona, to belt out the numbers on her blues harmonica. Polly did her best to keep up, but every song transitioned to instrumental improvisations under Kendell's unrelenting force.

The crowd was going wild. Kendell hadn't looked up since the music had taken possession of her, but halfway through the night, the screams and cheers from the teeming, dancing mass of humanity drowned out every diminished riff. In response to the energy they poured at the stage, her body felt like it became one with her instrument.

Covered in sweat and doing her best to control the saliva that threatened to leak out the corners of her mouth, she spotted Myles standing front and center in the audience. From deep within, she knew she should feel some inkling of embarrassment. But that night, she was raw feminine power, and he needed to succumb to her like the music that she continued to make her bitch.

As the band's three-hour set failed to adequately express Kendell's longing, the next band, The Mutants at Table Nine, joined Polly Urethane and the Strippers on stage. The raw, uncoordinated energy of multiple guitars, keyboards, and rhythm sections only drove the madness harder in Kendell. By the end of "Killing Floor," she had the cacophony rounded up like a border collie working a herd of sheep.

When she finally set her black guitar down after four hours of continual music, her fingertips were bleeding worse than they had during her earliest music classes. Looking down at the instrument, she realized she'd need new strings before their next gig.

Minerva hugged her tight. "Damn, girl, you were on fire up there."

Even Polly sounded ramped up. "Whatever shots of espresso you took before showing up tonight you need to bring for all of us next time. You were like a demon on stage."

The energy that had swept through her all night slowly

receded like the shadows running from the first rays of dawn. "I may have overdone it just a bit."

Lynn was still knocking the spit out of her harp. "Did you see those Mutants waiting to get on stage? I swear every one of those dudes had raging hard-ons. They weren't trying to take the stage from us. They just wanted in on the action."

Minerva hip-checked Kendell. "They weren't the only ones with erections. Did you see Myles trying to dance? That poor boy will be walking stiff-legged all night."

Scraper had been wiping the sweat off her axe. "You shouldn't tease him so hard. He seems like a decent person, for a guy."

As the adrenaline drained from Kendell's veins her muscles began to ache from the intense activity. "It's either drink until dawn or call it a night for me. Since I'll need to perfect that espresso recipe for Polly at work in a couple of hours, I think I'll head home."

Each of her bandmates gave her a bear hug before heading out. As Kendell secured her guitar back in its case, she felt heat coming from the small, zippered-shut side pocket. *Next time, you're staying at home.* If the tool had been the driving force of her playing, it wasn't a power she could control.

～

SHE KNEW the investigation had to continue, but after the Scratchy Dog session, she was grateful to have a few days of simple tasks like serving coffee at work and walking

Cheesecake when she got home. The tool was locked up with her important papers. And like her passport and health records, she didn't expect to pull it out again anytime soon.

She sat on her couch with both Cecile and her electric guitar out of their cases. Lovingly, she replaced all twelve stings. The black instrument never sounded as good as with a fresh set, but it would only take Cecile a few songs before the sound had mellowed to Kendell's liking. Cheesecake brought her fresh rawhide to the ottoman and began working it into the soft, disgusting kind of chew toy she preferred.

"I think I know how you felt in that warehouse, girl. I could have conquered the world last night, but I fear it would not have been to do good. No matter how hard the girls push me, don't let me pull it out for another gig, okay?"

Cheesecake continued chewing on her stick, but Kendell knew all she'd have to do was look at her dog and she'd remember. Neither of them needed to be further infected by that dark energy.

And as always, there was Myles. He'd attended nearly every gig she'd played that didn't conflict with his work schedule. But that night was different. She'd wanted him to see her in all her sexual power. He kept acting like some older brother intent on keeping her safe. She thought he would have to be gay for that to still be the case. Physical attraction, however, wasn't the same as wanting a romantic connection. She couldn't even answer the question of what she wanted. Partners, sex, romance, love—why did he have to be so damn confusing? She'd laid it all out on stage. If he wanted something more, he could damn well broach the subject like any horny male. As far as she was concerned, she would refocus her attention on the investigation. There was still work to be done.

Having come to grips with her emotions, she repacked her guitars in their cases. "I shouldn't be too late. You've got your stick to keep you busy."

In spite of the warming weather of late spring, she kept her coat with her as she and Myles silently walked the couple of blocks from the streetcar stop to the Laurette mansion. It might not be cold outside, but the house put a chill down her back. That was her reasoning, anyway. The coat was for warmth only, and the fact that it covered her body, which she'd so longed to show him under the power of the curse, was a side benefit. *Why am I feeling so embarrassed? We've shared so much.*

Samantha, in her Florence and the Machine 2012 concert-series T-shirt and ripped jeans, answered the door, looking happier than Kendell thought possible considering the recent death of Marilyn. "I'm glad you guys caught me. Come on in."

The last time they'd visited the old mansion Myles seemed reluctant to enter the house any farther than strictly necessary. After their psychic adventure she had a better understanding of why. To her the place looked like a mysterious building filled with hidden treasures and secret rooms, but to him it would be loaded up with generations of human energy. "The place looks considerably better than the last time we were here."

Samantha led them into the same office they'd visited before. "It's all for show. I gave up on the upstairs and attics.

By focusing my energy on the downstairs, I'm hoping to make this dump look appealing enough to sell. First impressions can do a lot to make prospective buyers overlook the skeletons in the closets, so long as that's only figuratively speaking."

Kendell had an urge to go wandering the upper rooms in search of the family's history. "Have you found anything of interest?"

"No more diaries, but I do have my grandfather's genealogical research ready for you." She pulled a stack of loose pages from the old desk. "I can't imagine what good they'll do you, but you're welcome to hang onto them for as long as you need. On the off chance that one day I do have kids and they want to know something about their family's history I guess I should ask for the family tree back when you're done. But I'm in no rush."

Kendell unfolded the first sheet of large graph paper. Names with connecting lines and dates were scribbled in every direction. Hoping for something more legible, she turned to the notepad. Under the heading Joseph Fouche were sections for physical description, occupation, dates of birth and death, and personal observations. That last heading made Kendell laugh. Under it, Samantha's grandfather had written, "Asshole wouldn't even let me past his secretary. Thinks a lot of himself for a public servant."

She tried to match up the name with the graph. "Your grandfather was quite thorough."

"Thoroughly disorganized. I spent a couple of hours last night trying to put the pieces together. He only put that standardized list of attributes together ten years before his death. The early pages are impossible to understand. His rambling observations were not complimentary."

Myles edged out toward the hallway. For a moment, Kendell thought he was looking to leave, but he pointed to the dining room. "Any chance we could use your dining table to lay all this stuff out? Neither of our apartments are big enough to really see this puzzle in its full glory."

"Not at all. I'd welcome the company. I doubt I'll be much use, but if you could use the help, I'd love a little distraction."

Kendell pulled her phone from her coat. "I'll order us some pizzas."

~

MYLES SAT on top of the six-foot ladder with a slice of pepperoni and mushroom pizza. His vantage point gave him a good view of the interlacing sheets of yellow legal pad and white graph paper that covered the ten-foot dining room table. "It's like a combination of a maze and modern art. I know I'm supposed to get something out of the installation, but it just looks like gibberish."

Kendell frowned up at him. "If you're not going to be helpful up there, you can come down and clean up the pizza boxes."

"Sorry, I was just making an observation." If he started on the long side of the table where Kendell was standing, the variety of last names and number of people was overwhelming. But at the other end was only the stack of pages describing the baron Archibald Batiste Malveaux.

Next to his information, where the paperwork for his wife should have been, was a lone sheet of blank yellow paper with a question mark on it. "How is it nothing is known about Mrs. Malveaux?"

Kendell turned back to the stack of pages. "I don't know. Even when we were looking up information on Serephine's death in the old newspapers, they didn't give her maiden name."

Samantha picked up the diary off the section of material about Antoine Caliste Malveaux. "As Anthony Laurette, Antoine mentioned that he wrote her frequently from the battlefield." She flipped to a section midway through the journal. "Here it is. 'Wrote Mother again today, but still unsure if nurses are giving her my letters. I try to assure her that I'm healthy if not safe, but with so much death around me, it might be better if my correspondences were kept from her. The poor old lady has suffered enough. I fear for what's left of her mind.'"

Myles pointed at a dividing line on the pages that ran through Antoine's name. "If the Civil War started in 1861, Antoine would have been about nineteen. It looks like the baron was in his fifties. Kendell, didn't your mother say something about Louis Broussard's daughter being your great-great-grandmother? That union must have been around the same time."

Kendell grabbed a sheet of paper and wrote what little was known about Serephine Malveaux. Birth: 1852, Death: 1860. "I know there's no way to be certain, but I believe she died right after the curse was cast. So that gives us a starting date for this nightmare of 1860. Mom said that after the baron lost his family, he spent all of his time in the brothels. Mrs. Malveaux had lost a daughter to suicide. Not long after that, her son joined the Confederate army. And her husband was so devious he sent his adversaries' families to work in his whorehouses. I'd guess she might not want to face those realities."

"What if when Antoine changed his name he took his mother's maiden name?" Myles asked. "He must have known that the baron's illegitimate children took their mothers' names. Perhaps he saw it as the ultimate insult."

Kendell wrote down Laurette on a small piece of paper and set it on the blank page reserved for the baron's wife. "If Anthony did, though, it wouldn't be a very good disguise from his father."

"I don't think he was trying to hide. If he were, New Orleans would be the last place he'd move to after the war. My guess is he wanted to show his father he could succeed without the old man's name, money, and connections. Anthony would want his true identity hidden from everyone *but* the baron."

Samantha leaned against the crumbling brick fireplace, drinking her beer. "But why would it matter? We're trying to figure out who killed Marilyn, and you're looking at family connections from a hundred and fifty years ago."

Myles jumped down from the ladder and made a couple of paper tabs marked "money," "power," "cursed items," and "Anthony's diaries." He put them all next to the paperwork about the baron. "We know eventually the cursed objects find their way to Anthony, based on the pipe tool being found in the wall here at the Laurette mansion." He moved that tab over to Anthony Laurette. "But Anthony would have rejected the old man's power and money. After the Civil War, the bank would have changed hands, but the baron's brothels, wealth, and political connections would have remained intact even if not out in the open. So where did they go after his death?"

Kendell climbed a couple of steps up the ladder. "I see a lot of powerful names on the opposite end of the table. The Laroque family boasts two of the last three mayors of New Orleans, the current chief of police, and a state senator."

From his position, it was hard to make out all the connections. "How far back does the name Laroque go before it intersects Laurette?"

"Anthony Laurette had four children. The oldest daughter, Fleurentine, married Marcus Laroque."

Myles reached across the table and picked up the sheet of paper marked Fleurentine Laurette. He stared at the names, imagining Anthony's anger at his father. "She was called Phiny but not because of her first name. Her middle name was Serephine. I know it's reaching, but you don't suspect that Fleurentine was Antoine's mother's name, do you? In his firstborn daughter, he might have sought to enshrine the memory of the two women he most loved and whom he thought his father had destroyed."

Samantha wrote "Fleurentine" next to "Laurette" on the page next to the baron. "So we finally meet the woman."

Kendell pointed at the page in Myles's hand. "When does it say Anthony's daughter lived?"

"1866–1948. She married Marcus in 1892. They had three children. The eldest, Nathan Laroque, was the first to attain political office. He was mayor of New Orleans from 1924 to 1934, serving four terms." Myles grabbed sheet after sheet describing the heirs of Anthony's first-born daughter. "Looks like after Nathan, the Laroque family dug firmly into New Orleans politics."

Samantha picked up the folder describing Laura Laroque. "A dynasty that continues to this day. Laura just won her second term as our state senator. But again, I don't see what any of this has to do with Marilyn's murder."

"I do." Kendell jumped down and ran around the table to the tabs Myles had written. "First Anthony insults his father by naming his first born after the two women. Then the baron retaliates by corrupting Marcus Laroque or Fleurentine or both. Do you remember those pictures we saw of the Laurette family? They weren't rich. Anthony might have made a name for himself as an architect, but that would have taken decades. So unless Marcus came from money, the Laroque family needed someone with wealth and connections to start their political dynasty."

Myles consulted the pages. "It's possible. The baron died in 1893. Fleurentine had already married Marcus."

Kendell placed the tabs marked "power" and "money" on the section of the table-sized chart occupied by Fleurentine Laurette-Laroque. "That cunning bastard. The baron's ultimate revenge on his son was to turn his daughter into everything Anthony had tried to escape."

Samantha tossed her beer bottle in the trash. "You two have quite the active imaginations. Next you're going to tell me the Laroque family still runs the old brothels."

Myles picked up the remaining tab marked "Anthony's

diaries." "It's just a hypothesis. But somewhere on this table is the name of the person who killed Marilyn. Anthony Laurette believed in the Malveaux curse enough to seek out his half siblings, like Kendell's grandpapas, to warn them. If he did that for relative strangers, he must have told the story to his own children until they had it memorized. They wouldn't have needed the diaries, but as a final warning to Fleurentine's family, he might have left the journals to her children." Myles consulted the dates of births and deaths. "Anthony would have lived just long enough to see Nathan Laroque become mayor. How much do you want to bet that's where the diaries ended up?"

Samantha brought in a fresh round of beers from the kitchen. "Well, the story wasn't widely discussed around our dinner table."

Kendell took a long drink of her Abita Amber. "Your family left New Orleans. And your father was suspicious of you returning. Most of the old families down here don't hold with the superstitions of their elders. Assuming the curse involved some of the baron's personal possessions, and considering that the pipe tool was found in the wall here, I'd guess Anthony did what he could to hide the objects. But he couldn't be sure he'd gotten them all." She walked around the table to the sheet of paper headlined Marilyn Fontenot 1973–2017. "She lived her whole life down here. She would have heard about the curse, possibly from her grandparents. Samantha, if your grandfather put together a family tree, maybe her family did something similar. I know our hypothesis is filled with ifs, but if

Marilyn thought she'd found a big story, it might have put her in danger."

$\sim$

KENDELL RUBBED her eyes as she and Myles walked back to the streetcar. "I love investigating old documents, but that old man's handwriting sucked. It was nice of Samantha to let us take the pages home with us. We already took up an entire afternoon of her time poring over her family tree." As the day had worn on, Kendell felt a growing sense of obligation toward every person listed in the genealogy.

Myles had the old laptop bag slung over his shoulder. But instead of a computer, it was filled with the paperwork that had been carefully compiled from Samantha's dining table. "I get the impression she'll be happy to see the last of New Orleans and her family legacy. She's very sweet, but she reminds me of your mother. What did your dad call her —an emotional tumbleweed?"

Kendell held her heavy coat in her arms and enjoyed the late afternoon sunlight that filtered through the trees to her face. "I hope she stays. I like her. But you're probably right."

"You know, if it is the Laroque family, we're in way over our heads."

She could tell he was feeling her out again on her commitment to the investigation. "We don't know anything yet. I want to see Marilyn's notes on what she was working on. Since her job with the *Picayune* was just writing fluff personal-interest stories, I suspect that's where our adventure will end. Since no one else is looking into her death, we owe it to her to do what we can."

"And if her notes do lead somewhere?"

She knew neither one of them could stand up against Chief of Police Gerald Laroque or State Senator Laura Laroque. "We don't even qualify as David versus Goliath. In spite of our paranormal connections, there's no invisible, all-powerful being standing on our side. The Laroque family could crush us without leaving a clue. Just like they did to Marilyn."

"We have a few advantages she lacked. The curse not only doesn't work on you, but you may be one of the few people who can defeat it. We may not have many allies, but I suspect both Professor Yates and Madam de Galpion are well connected to the paranormal underworld. And we have the most fearsome hellhound known to man."

Kendell snickered at his joke. "That's true. Cheesecake, defender of the underdog."

"Have you accessed that dark-web forum Link told us about?"

"Yep. He vouched for me like he said he would. The post about the theft listed the job as complete. A lot of pilferers are hailing Lion—that's Link's screen name—as a master thief. Whoever commissioned the job left a short but positive review. Otherwise, it's been quiet. I haven't seen any posts about looking for more Malveaux objects."

Myles pulled out some money for the streetcar. "Any mention of the pipe tool itself?"

"No. Both Link and the person who made the request kept quiet about it. There was no mention of wanting it again. If we're right about the Laroque family, maybe they think it's safely in police storage. Or maybe they just don't care if all they were after was Marilyn's death."

He helped her onto one of the old, highly lacquered wooden seats. "Have you made any posts?"

Even if she hadn't recently experienced a shared mental connection with him, she'd have known when he was being overly protective. "And risk you yelling at me? I think not."

"Just trying to figure out if I get to sleep tonight or if I should keep the phone handy for your cry of help."

She suppressed her initial response of telling him he could stay at her place just in case. Some jokes hit a little too close to home. If anything romantic were to develop, she didn't want it to be with her as the girl always in need of rescue. The only relationship she could accept would be one of equals.

17

*M*yles couldn't take his eyes off Kendell. In her backless black dress and high-heeled shoes, all of her curves were perfectly displayed. Part of him felt bad for so blatantly admiring his friend's beauty, but if she had wanted him to maintain the girl-next-door impression of her, she probably wouldn't have accepted his invitation to the Endymion Ball in the first place. "You look amazing."

She gave him a half twirl that made the dress fly up to her knees. "Thank you, kind sir." The coquette only lasted for a moment. "I can't believe you got tickets. Dance with me?"

He took her hand and led her into the high-society throng. Dances had never been his thing in school, and the drunk tourists who frequented the bar didn't make the activity seem any more inviting. But with every person in the Super Dome so elegantly dressed, he wondered what he'd been missing. Even finding a reasonable space to dance wasn't an issue.

Kendell's moves reminded him of seeing her on stage with Polly Urethane and the Strippers. Instead of grinding and flirting for the entire audience, this time her moves were just for him. As if knowing she had his full attention, she put her hands on her head and shimmied her body just far enough from him so that he could see her every move. Most women he dated were so overly confident in their beauty that they didn't feel it necessary to do much more than stand there. Kendell undulated like an exotic belly dancer enticing a rich patron. He leaned in close. "I never knew you had these kinds of moves."

She slipped her hands from her head to his shoulders so she could talk in his ear. "Get us quiet ones out of our shells, and we'll surprise you every time."

They were still partners. That wasn't something he wanted to endanger. But Mardi Gras Balls were closer to masquerade than reality. He put his hands on her sides and pulled her closer. She teased her breasts and hips against him. But before anything became too serious, she laughed and moved away. "I could go for something to drink."

He suspected she too felt the tension of sexual attraction competing with their mission. "Chardonnay?"

She batted her long eyelashes at him. "You remembered."

"Stay here. I don't want to lose you. I'll be right back."

The crowd was still filling the huge space prior to the arrival of the parade floats and marching bands. He'd have to hold her close when the party really kicked into full gear. As always seemed to be the case, the bar was the first to experience the incoming throng of people. But Myles had an in. "Hey, Charlie, thanks for the tickets. Can I get a beer and a chardonnay?"

"You got it. Anytime you want to work one of these events, I can land you the gig." Charlie looked out across the bobbing heads. "Once these socialites get a little tipsy, it's an amazing place to pick up chicks. Even better than the bar on Bourbon Street. These women stay classy no matter how intoxicated they get. Once the parade floats arrive, it'll be full-on Carnival."

Myles took the drinks, grateful he didn't have to wait half an hour just to get the bartender's attention. Women who were laughing and flirting filled in the area around him. All he wanted, though, was to get back to Kendell. "Have fun, my friend."

"I always do."

Myles had to squeeze past a couple of groupings of college kids, but he found his way back to the pillar where he'd left Kendell with little trouble. He searched the crowd before spotting her dancing with a man their age in a garish purple-and-gold suit. She looked to be having fun but was keeping a greater distance from her new dance partner than she had with him.

As the warm-up group on stage ended their song, he moved in to catch her attention. Before he could, however, she was whisked deeper into the crowd for another song. Myles could handle letting his date go for a single dance, but this guy was beginning to put his moves on her—as well as his hands. Instead of allowing her the space to move as she pleased, her dance partner felt it necessary to pull her tight to his grinding hips.

Myles saw the brilliance of cutting in, but with his hands full of drinks, dancing would be out. Still, he couldn't stand idly by and watch his friend get pawed at by some letch who didn't know his place. As his fear grew that he might have to physically intervene, he saw her put an unusual dance move on her partner. Instead of gyrating her hips with his, she bent her knee up sharply between his legs. He didn't double over, but she had clearly made her message understood.

Myles held out the glass of white wine as she flipped her hair back at the guy, who was still struggling to stand upright. "Nice move. Remind me not to get too frisky on the dance floor with you."

"He had it coming. That was Lance Laroque. He was in my freshman English class in college. Honestly, I didn't think he knew who I was back then. No sooner had you gone to get us drinks than he moved in and practically demanded we dance. He hasn't changed at all since school. Even back then, he thought every woman just fell at his feet. That dude has a serious case of the entitlements."

As she snuggled up close to him, he felt a warm glow knowing that when it came to overtures from other guys, she could take care of herself. "So that's one of the Laroque family."

She pointed toward a boisterous table near where the floats would be arriving. "That's the less well-off branch of the family. The rich and powerful Laroques either ride on the Grand Marshal's float or have a reserved space near the stage."

He tossed his empty bottle into the trash and grabbed her around the waist. "Fuck 'em. Tonight, I just want to dance with you and catch fancy stuffed toys for Cheesecake to rip to shreds later."

By the time the first marching band entered the arena, he'd forgotten all about the Laroques and their arrogance. The bright, colorful strobe lights from the floats lit up Kendell's dark-brown eyes as she anticipated receiving the thrown items that sailed through the air. Even the rich and elegant people who surrounded them couldn't deny the excitement of catching meaningless plastic beads and Mardi Gras paraphernalia. More than once, he lifted her by the waist to catch some shiny bobble that all those around her yearned for.

~

KENDELL FOUND people in New Orleans more open during Mardi Gras. Something about the parades, food, and overall excitement lowered the social barriers. Even so, she was surprised when Marilyn's brother accepted their request to discuss what she'd been working on. Having Samantha vouch for them had done wonders.

The renovated shotgun double in the Uptown neighborhood made her imagine a different life for herself. If her mother wasn't an emotional tumbleweed... if her parents hadn't divorced... if she'd gone to school with these people who were now pushing baby strollers and weeding their front gardens, who would she be? She wanted to believe such a privileged upbringing would have made her a social activist. She'd be the one championing the rights of those less well-off. But looking around at the peaceful neighborhood, she imagined such luxury had a way of insulating these happy individuals from the suffering of others. It wasn't an upbringing she desired. Cheesecake would be barking like a fool at every passing poodle. And Kendell doubted she'd have had the opportunity to meet Myles.

A man in his midforties, wearing slacks and a cotton shirt that was too well tailored to be inexpensive, answered the door. "You're Samantha's friends? Come on in. I don't know what we can do for you. We're still in shock over Marilyn's death."

Before entering the house, Kendell spotted the black wreath on the other door to the double. "Thank you for seeing us. I'm so sorry for your loss. Samantha has such nice things to say about her distant cousin."

"Samantha's a sweetheart. I'm Alfred, and this is my wife, Anna. I am—was—Marilyn's brother."

Kendell took Myles's hand and sat on the reproduction antique settee. "We don't want to intrude, but we had some questions about your sister and what she was working on."

"Samantha told us. I'm happy to tell you anything you'd like to know, but I will warn you, the whole thing about our family being cursed isn't something we believe in. So if your intention is to bring up a bunch of hocus-pocus, we'll have to ask you to leave. Marilyn's death was an accident. We don't need people turning it into something it wasn't."

"I understand." Not long ago, Kendell would have had the same reaction. "What can you tell us about your sister?"

"You know the popular kids in high school? Marilyn would have been their queen, though she was never arrogant about it. I was the nerdy kid brother. But instead of trying to hide me from her friends and pretend I didn't exist, she continually tried to work me into her clique. Every birthday or Christmas, she'd buy me expensive, fashionable clothes. She introduced me to the younger girls who tried to join the inner circle of popular kids, hoping one of them would take a liking to me. Marilyn never gave up on me. In spite of our vast differences, we were very close."

Kendell hoped if she'd had a brother she would have been as caring. "She sounds very kind."

Anna's restrained laugh matched the conservative décor. "She wasn't, at least not to those outside of her circle. She just had a soft spot for Freddie. I guess you haven't read any of her society columns."

Alfred gave his wife a sorrowful smile. "School was a long time ago. But Anna's right. Marilyn had a biting satire. It's what made her articles on New Orleans high society so titillating. She never really outgrew that popular-girl image. As those around her found financial success one way or another, Marilyn found writing about their exploits could keep her the center of attention. If there was a high-class party, she'd be there. I once joked that she never married because a husband would put too much of a kink in her nightlife."

Myles squirmed against the slick fabric. She knew he was feeling out of his element. "Sounds like she had a pretty good life."

"She did, but after she turned forty, she started wondering if there was more to life than reporting on the latest gossip. For the last few years, she'd tried to convince the paper to give her something real to report on, but the news doesn't work that way. They told her to go out and find a story and they'd consider it. Unfortunately, hard-hitting journalism wasn't her forte."

Kendell tried to keep the excitement out of her voice. "Was she working on anything interesting?"

Alfred pulled out a set of keys. "I haven't had the heart to enter her side of the house. I can't imagine there are any family skeletons that she would have been mortified of anyone discovering. All I'd ask is that you be respectful while you're in her home, and let me see anything you discover."

"Are you sure?" Kendell asked. "I really don't want to impose."

Anna took the keys from her husband. "I'll go with you if it makes you more at ease. I can show you her office and unlock her computer."

After entering the darkened side of the shotgun house, Kendell put her coat back on. "Is it colder in here or just my emotional response?"

Myles wrapped his arm around her shoulder and pulled her close. "It's like her presence is still here."

They stood in the living room as Anna went through the place turning on the lights and opening the curtains. The furnishings were less ostentatious than those on the other side of the shared wall. Two comfortable-looking lounge chairs bordered the fireplace with a small writer's table between them. Kendell picked up a newspaper and saw Marilyn had circled the Mardi Gras party that had preceded her fateful parade.

Anna returned from the back of the house. "I booted up her computer. There's still some sodas in the fridge. Please help yourself. Marilyn was a stickler for offering beverages to her guests. You'd be honoring her by making yourselves at home. I'll stay here in the living room, if you don't mind, just to answer any questions. Alfred is still an emotional wreck. It'll make him feel better knowing I'm here."

Kendell set the paper back on the table. "We'd feel better knowing you're here too. Is there anything we can do or find for you while we're poking around?"

"Marilyn was more sister to me than sister-in-law. Living so close together made us good friends. I know her house and possessions almost as well as I know my own. As you can see, she was a very tidy person. Just put things back where you find them, and I know she'll rest easy."

Kendell smiled to herself, knowing the dead woman would have someone so dear to her in her house while strangers poked around her possessions. "We should be able to find everything we're looking for in her office, unless you know of any family history she might have stashed away in some closet."

"Don't we all have boxes of papers and family heirlooms stashed away somewhere? I'll have a look in her bedroom while you two check her computer files. Freddy might have some stuff in our attic as well. It'll give him something to do other than fret about the noises coming from his sister's rooms."

While Kendell searched through the computer emails, Myles started opening boxes from the office closet. "Apparently, she had a thing for high-school yearbooks. There must be a hundred different schools represented on these shelves."

"Makes sense. Most people form friendships and enemies in high school that last all their lives. Is there any organization to her collection?"

He set a couple of the heavy boxes in the middle of the room. "Actually, it's very organized. There's very little dust on the books that are out on the shelves, and even the ones in boxes look like they were frequently consulted. She's got Post-Its throughout each book." He opened a couple and laid them next to each other. "She color coded the couples who hooked up from different schools. The woman was very detail oriented. Any luck with the computer?"

"So far, just old articles she'd written. There's a ton of information. It almost reminds me of looking at Samantha's genealogical chart, but this is all recent history intermixed with social events and gossip. This is going to take a while."

After three hours of reading about marriages, divorces, marital dalliances, and social power plays, Kendell felt like she'd lost more than enough brain cells for one day. "This is impossible. I can't for the life of me see what important news story she thought she'd found."

She turned the office chair and saw that Myles had covered the floor in open yearbooks. "There's a pattern here. I just can't quite see it. A lot of the unions are what I'd expect—popular girls marrying jocks, nerds marrying geeks —but there's also a thread of connections that don't make sense. It's almost like the families were trying to consolidate their power. Maybe I've been spending too much time thinking about conspiracies."

Kendell pointed to a line of yearbooks that ran down the middle of the room to the door. "That's the Laroque family?"

"I thought it made the most sense to put them in the middle, but I'm not seeing anything we didn't already know."

Kendell blushed on seeing her mother's picture. "And that's my family over against the wall?"

"Just your mother and Grammy. Having sort of met your grandmother in your memory, I wish I'd known her in person. From the entries in the yearbook, it looks like she was kind of a partier in her day."

"What's the oldest yearbook Marilyn had in her collection?" Seeing pictures and reading quotes from long-dead people recorded on paper was more interesting than reading recent emails.

"She's got some going back to the late 1920s."

Kendell stood and carefully walked around the layer of yearbooks. From all the faces a pattern started to emerge. "Look at the long noses and tight mouths on so many of these people Marilyn tagged. The last names don't match up, but if I were just to meet them on the street, I'd swear they were related."

"That's what I was missing. I was so busy focusing on the names I didn't look closely enough at the pictures. I'd recognize that smug asshole look anywhere. Lance Laroque really is a chip off the family block, isn't he?" Myles got up from his squatting position and grabbed a couple of books from beneath the others. "The connecting names are all old New Orleans families. Like there was some common ancestor."

Kendell felt her blood run cold. "The baron Archibald Baptiste Malveaux. I'll bet anything these people were descended from women who'd been taken into indentured servitude like my great-great-great-grandmother."

"It's hard to believe so many families would have reestablished themselves in only a couple of generations. Not everyone made it as far as high school in the first half of the twentieth century. And these kids don't look like they came from poor families."

Kendell balled her fists at what she was thinking. "Presumably, my ancestor who lost his family to the baron died. Suppose these other families didn't lose their fathers? After they'd served their time and had children from the baron they would have been returned to their homes."

"He cemented himself into their legacies. The families would still be struggling. By lending them more money, he wouldn't just be rebuilding New Orleans after the Civil War—he'd be making them all beholden to him. And if they ever needed reminding of who was in charge of the city or what happens to those who displease him, all they'd have to do is look at their children or those of their neighbors. Look at the marriages through the generations. Those with the baron's attributes married up, consolidating their wealth and power. Their cousins who shared the same surnames but not the same attributes—in other words, the children of the indentured women and their husbands—didn't fare as well. The baron's reach continues to this day, according to these yearbooks."

Kendell worked her way back to the desk with a renewed mission. "You don't suppose that's what Marilyn was on to?"

"Now that I see the connection, I don't know how it's something she would have missed. New Orleans' dirty history. I doubt that's an article many of the upper class would want to see published."

She started printing out every wedding notification that had been forwarded to Marilyn from the area newspapers. "It's not just about the past. Those families owed both financial and personal debts to the baron Malveaux, who might have handed the ledger to his granddaughter, thus creating the Laroque dynasty. Why else would he want a visual human record that would transcend generations?"

"You think tying the Laroque's rise to power to the city's dark secret is what got Marilyn killed?"

"I think they'd see her article as a betrayal of an heir to the true Malveaux bloodline. Family members turn on no one more viciously than the person who reveals their family's dirty laundry. Especially if that family is of the powerful upper class."

Myles began closing up the yearbooks and returning them to their boxes. "All the more reason for the Laroques to keep information of the curse out of the hands of anyone not related to Anthony Laurette. At least their relatives would be in equal danger."

Kendell helped him load the heavy boxes back in the closet. She'd originally dismissed the pile of newspapers and magazines that leaned against the wall as light reading material. She accidentally knocked the pile over and stared at the highlighted wedding announcement. "Apparently, the Laroques have higher aspirations than just New Orleans. Look at this. 'Bradford Baptiste Laroque, president of the Harvard Law Review, to marry Kennedy granddaughter.' I'll bet this pile is loaded with similar announcements."

He started thumbing through the pile with her. "Someone in the family is trying to whitewash the past before making a play for national office."

"With a power base going back generations, you don't really believe it's just one person, do you?"

18

*M*yles's first reaction on seeing Lance Laroque enter the bar on Bourbon Street was to want to toss the creep into the gutter. But a bad reputation regarding the city's powerful family would mean an end to his bartending career. "What can I get you?" *that will include a spit shot.*

"I'm not here to make trouble. If you want Kendell, be my guest. I was just trying to talk to her at the ball."

Right. "About what?"

"If you're working with her on investigating my family, you're both in danger. People who cross the Laroques have a way of going missing."

Myles considered throwing the shot glass at him but continued cleaning it with the rag. "That sounds a lot like a threat."

He pulled out a card with an address. "Send Kendell. The nuns don't like letting men into their convent. Have her ask for any information they have on Fleurentine Laurette. If you find it useful, I'd like to hear anything you know about my family. I'm not asking you to trust me."

Myles picked up the card, which was for Our Lady of Mercy Convent. "And I'm supposed to believe anything they say?"

"I'm not going to bullshit you. I'm not a nice guy. My family's rich, powerful, and moving up the political ladder. But that doesn't mean I'm okay with standing by while people get hurt. Have Kendell check with the nuns. At the very least, they'll vouch for me. Then meet me at Scratch and Sniff at one in the morning on Friday."

Myles didn't consider himself a fool. "First you threaten me, then you expect me to meet you in some dark shop in the middle of the night?"

"I was just looking for neutral ground. I know you've met with Madam de Galpion. With you working nights, I figured later would be better for you. If you don't like my suggestion, come up with one of your own."

Kendell had felt safe at the perfumery, and he suspected Madam de Galpion knew more than she'd let on. Another trip to the shop wasn't the worst idea. "Scratch and Sniff is okay, but let's make it one in the afternoon."

"Suit yourself. She doesn't usually open during the day, but she will for me." The arrogant asshole left to rejoin the crowd of revelers that grew by the day as Fat Tuesday approached.

Charlie spun a couple of bottles of beer down the bar toward two waiting customers in front of Myles. "Friend of yours?"

"Not likely. Ever hear of Our Lady of Mercy Convent?"

"Sure. It's behind that big wall that takes up a city block of the French Quarter. Fucking waste of space, but anything that historic isn't going anywhere."

Myles studied the card again for anything other than the name and address. "Any reason why they would have taken in people suffering from mental illness?"

Charlie worked around him to grab a bottle of expensive tequila. "After the Civil War, that's where a lot of people ended up if the hospitals could no longer help. Study some history once in a while, but for now, get some drinks for those girls batting their eyes at you."

~

THE OLD NUN who greeted Kendell at the front gate of Our Lady of Mercy Convent had a kindly face, though Kendell suspected her piercing steely-blue eyes could penetrate any deception. "We aren't open to the public."

Kendell imagined the old woman must get pestered on a daily basis by tourists looking to explore the old grounds. "Lance Laroque sent me. I'm here about Fleurentine Laurette."

The mention of the names deepened the lines across the woman's forehead. "If you feel it necessary to invade our sanctuary, I must ask that you keep quiet until we reach my office."

As the heavy wooden gate shut behind her, a feeling of calm came over Kendell. Her emotions perfectly matched the silence from the outside world maintained by the heavy masonry walls that encompassed the grounds. Though her life of excitement and adventure thrilled her, just for a moment, she could appreciate the quiet, contemplative life of the nuns. Seeing all the women studiously tending the gardens, reading, and performing their daily devotionals gave her a perspective she hadn't anticipated.

But it wasn't just the street noise and Kendell's emotions that were quieted. The energy that had permeated her like a subwoofer set so low it could be felt more than heard softened as well. Only in the spiritual quiet of the convent could she identify the tool's continual effect on her. The journey she'd shared with Myles to their childhoods and the curse's origin had allowed the tool to mesh with her soul. She wasn't cursed, but the driving force was unmistakable. *If this is just a taste of power, no wonder the Laroques are so addicted to gaining more.*

The nun's office was much as Kendell expected. It was modest in its furnishings, quiet, and filled with light from the large window that looked out at the garden. The woman pointed to a well-used wooden chair. "Please have a seat. As I said at the gate, we're not open to the public. The Laroque family, however, has been very generous in keeping us afloat. So certain concessions are granted where they are concerned. Mr. Lance did mention you may be paying us a visit. He's already removed the unfortunate woman's diaries and correspondences, though."

"Did he take anything else?"

The woman sat behind her oak desk. "No. He only wanted her documents. He asked about her other possessions, but his questions weren't appropriate for our religious community."

Kendell knew she had to tread lightly. Anything she said could have her escorted out of the convent. "Did he think something of Fleurentine's might be cursed?"

"We are a deeply religious order. The ideas of evil, dark magic, and curses are left at the gate. Though we accept their existence, we choose a higher direction for our lives." The old nun pulled out a folder with Fleurentine Laurette written across the cover. "From the writings of my predecessor, Mrs. Malveaux was a very disturbed individual. Her marriage and children were well known to the church, of course. As the Malveaux family was part of high society, all of their major life events like marriages, christenings, and deaths were conducted at Saint Louis Cathedral. She never forgave the church, however, for denying little Serephine a proper church burial due to her suicide. But Miss Fleur, as she was known in the convent, renounced her previous life once she entered our grounds."

"She became a nun?" That wasn't something Kendell had expected.

"No. Her mind was too far gone, but it helped keep her calm to imagine she was one of us and not just one of our charges. I mention her history so you'll have a better understanding of how she viewed her possessions. Mr. Lance expressed concern that once Archibald Malveaux died, some of his things might have found their way here. According to this record, there was an attempt at delivering a box, but Miss Fleur wanted nothing to do with it."

Kendell found it hard to imagine the woman's state of

mind at hearing of the baron's death. She must have wanted to turn her back on everything associated with her marriage. "So none of the baron's belongings are here at the convent?"

"Just because Miss Fleur refused delivery, that didn't mean the box wasn't included in her list of possessions at her death. This is a very large compound. Our storage rooms would rival a good-sized warehouse."

Kendell knew she'd imposed enough on the nun's patience. "I can imagine. There's no need to go digging for her possessions. The objects are probably best left in your care."

"I appreciate your consideration. I only wish Mr. Lance had felt the same way about her documents."

~

A FAINT BLUE haze drifted out the top of Madam de Galpion's shop door as Kendell and Myles entered. The smell of tannins and fresh-baked bread made Kendell remember childhood Christmas dinners. "Why do you think he wanted to meet here?"

Myles rubbed his eyes. "Maybe he wanted to poison us with this smoke."

"My apologies for the intensity." Madam de Galpion emerged from the back room wearing a long, flowing dress printed in geometric shapes that reminded Kendell of Africa. "The incenses are of my making. They will help keep everyone calm, truthful, and hopefully cooperative."

Kendell gripped the pipe tool in her pocket and felt its

power radiate to her soul. She still wasn't convinced the meeting was a good idea. "How do you know Lance Laroque?"

Madam de Galpion lit another candle on her desk. "Generations of his family have been customers of my people. He has a passion to understand the paranormal. Unlike many, he's mostly interested in preventing harm. I wouldn't trust him if I were you, but you have more in common than you might suspect."

The way Lance held his chin almost perpendicular to his neck as he entered the shop made it appear that he was looking down on everyone. "I'm not on your side. This is a business meeting and nothing else. You have information that I want. You are also in possession of the baron's pipe tool."

Kendell seethed in her chair. "So that's it. You're after the cursed object."

"Don't be stupid. I wouldn't dare touch that thing. I don't even like being in the same room with it. But just because I find its use repugnant doesn't mean the same is true for other members of my family."

Myles exchanged a look of confusion with Kendell. "Then what do you want?"

Lance shook his head in apparent disgust. "You think it's so easy, don't you? I'm a *Laroque*. Wealth, power, and success just fall from the heavens and into my arms. Such bullshit. We're like the lion pride living among the animals of the savanna. You all think we're just preying on you, but none of you have any idea what it's like to be in the family. The elders are constantly pitting us against each other to search out the strongest and most ambitious. Those lucky few that are deemed worthy are given the keys to the kingdom, sent to the best schools, married to the most prominent families, and groomed for greatness. But what do you think happens to those of us who don't measure up?"

While in school, Kendell had wondered why Lance was the only Laroque at Southeastern Louisiana State, but it wasn't a contemplation that occupied much of her attention. "You seem to be doing all right."

"What you call all right, I call purgatory. But you're missing my point. We're bred to be competitive and to win at all costs. I'm no different. What strengthens the family is all that matters. But using curses and killing our opposition within the family are signs of weakness. Such actions are beneath us."

As Kendell held the tool in her pocket, she could feel its hatred for every one of the Laroque family. "You expect us to help you weed out whoever killed Marilyn?"

"Not without compensation. I know you have questions about my family. I won't give any answers that will harm our future, but I can direct you toward information about the past."

Myles kept his hand on the satchel with the copies of Samantha's family tree. "It might surprise you to know we're not all that interested in the Laroque family. Not everyone is enamored with you people."

For all of Lance's bravado, his ability to keep his anger in check impressed Kendell. "No, but you are interested in the Malveaux curse." He pulled out a small black notebook and tossed it on the table. Written across the front in gold lettering was the name Fleurentine Laurette.

As Myles reached for the notebook, Lance slammed his fist onto the cover. "Not so fast. I'll take the Laurette family history first if you don't mind."

Myles put the canvas bag on the table. "They're copies. We edited out anything that would lead directly to Samantha's grandfather as the compiler. If any harm comes to her, we'll see that you're the prime suspect."

Lance let out a dismissive single-syllable laugh. "My uncle is the chief of police. Your threats are pathetic."

Madam de Galpion had remained quietly at her desk until the transfer had been complete. "In the interest of everyone's safety, I'd suggest you all conduct your research here then hand back the documents. Even photocopies can be incriminating. I only vouch for the exchange of information, not possessions."

Kendell handled the diary as if it were in the Historic New Orleans Collection's library. From the brittleness of the pages, she suspected it hadn't been handled in many years. "I wish I had some cotton gloves. This thing should really be preserved."

Lance was in the process of covering every available surface with pages from the family tree. "A couple of pages fell out while I was looking at it. Other than a lot of motherly sentimentality, I thought the woman had lost her mind. Just a bunch of semicoherent ramblings in my opinion."

At least Myles had the good sense to keep his hands off the document. The journal was written less like a daily diary than a summation of her life. "She was only fifteen when she married Archibald Baptiste Malveaux. Her description of their courtship sounds less like falling madly in love than being emotionally manipulated."

Myles made notes as she talked. "How old was the baron?"

"He wasn't a baron at that time. She says he was ten years her senior, so twenty-five years old."

Myles tapped his pen on his notebook. "Does she say anything about him becoming baron? From what we heard about his banking career, it sounded like he already had the title."

She lifted the front and back cover to carefully advance a handful of pages into the history. As she read, she let go of the book to keep from damaging it accidentally. "It wasn't an English title. According to Fleurentine, he considered himself to be the heir of Baron Samedi, a Haitian voodoo loa of the dead."

Madam de Galpion lit her pipe and added the smell of exotic tobacco to the haze of incense. "Baron Samedi is a powerful figure in voodoo culture. He's known for his debauchery, rude language, and fondness for women. If Archibald Malveaux followed Samedi's example so closely he convinced the good people of New Orleans to refer to him as baron, he would have been an intimidating presence."

"How did Fleurentine take to his self-proclaimed title?" Myles asked.

Kendell carefully scanned a few pages seeking answers. "They'd been married a couple of years. She was entering her late teens. She makes him sound very debonair but also arrogant to the point of social recklessness. There's a lot of talk about parties, observations about the powerful people around them, and social connections the new baron wanted to make. It all sounds very calculated."

Lance looked up from his studies. "Of course it was. Look at the family now. Where do you think we got the drive to succeed?"

She really didn't want to engage him only to hear the merits of greed and selfishness. "Fleurentine talks about some of the sheer dresses he bought for her, imported from France. He insisted she forgo the usual undergarments in order to titillate those he hoped to impress. It doesn't sound like she minded the attention."

"I would guess that changed when she started having kids."

Kendell only had to skip one page. "She wasn't even twenty when Antoine was born. Most of the next few pages are about him growing up. There's hardly any mention of her husband. It's almost as if she didn't want to know what he was up to. If she did find out, she didn't write about it."

"Does she write much about Serephine?"

Kendell kept reading but with an eye for any further mention of the baron. "Her description of their family life makes it sound like it consisted of a single mother and her two children. There's a nanny, of course, but Fleurentine talks about her children as if they're her whole life."

She turned the page to see a black border had been drawn around the two pages. Myles made a note about it. "What do you suppose that's about?"

"It's the death of Serephine. The handwriting is really jagged and hard to read. You don't suppose that's when she had her mental breakdown?"

Lance piled a bunch of the pages to make room for his next stack. "Keep reading. I don't want to spoil the story."

Kendell did what she could to make out the writing. "She talks about the curse. I think that's Marie Laveau, but the letters are nearly on top of each other." She turned the page to see hellish images of demons surrounding what she recognized as the pipe tool. "I can't read any more. You take it—just be careful."

Myles looked nearly in shock as she passed the journal to him. "Are you sure?"

"It's like those demons aren't just on the page. I can almost feel them." Kendell knew it was silly to imagine drawings from over a hundred years ago coming to life. But then, she did share a family bond with Fleurentine.

Myles read in silence for a few pages. "She spends some time talking about Antoine after Serephine's death. He met with Marie Laveau. Either he didn't get much information or didn't want to tell his mother what he'd learned. There are some references to the Cursed Devil. She writes the word with the same flourishes she used for 'baron,' so I'd guess she's talking about her husband."

"Does she say when she entered Our Lady of Mercy?"

Kendell smiled at how carefully Myles handled the book. "About six months after Serephine died. Just before Antoine joined the Confederate army. From her weakening handwriting, I'd guess losing her only son was the last straw for her sanity."

Kendell had trouble writing the notes as she envisioned the poor woman being left so completely alone. "She couldn't have been older than her midthirties. Does she mention receiving Antoine's letters from the war?"

"Yep. She confirms Antoine and Anthony are the same person. She writes that he told her once the war was over, he was going to devote himself to making right his father's sins while still protecting the family. I'm afraid there's not much of any use after that. She writes a lot about the flowers in the garden, how nice the nuns are to her, and how she hopes she never has to face life outside the convent walls again."

Kendell tossed her notebook on the table. "Great. Another interesting historic tidbit with no new information."

Lance stacked the remaining pages of the Laurette family tree. "I didn't say it'd be useful."

As always, she wanted to smack the smug look off his face. "Did you find anything useful in what we provided?"

"I didn't say anything about sharing what I've discovered. But if it puts your mind at ease, I think I now know what I'm up against. There's a faction of my family that would like to take control before it's too late. Once the current power base gets one of their members elected to national office, there won't be a way to stop them."

Kendell again held the tool in her pocket. "What did Marilyn have to do with it?"

Lance folded up his notes. "She trusted the wrong friend. I told you before, questioning the Laroques can get you killed even if you're not making accusations. Since I am not among the powerful or power hungry, I'll offer you this one piece of advice. Get rid of that pipe tool you've got in your pocket. You thought I didn't know you had it with you? If you keep it, someone in my family will use you like a pawn, just like they did Marilyn. They got the information they wanted from her. Then they disposed of her so she wouldn't talk."

Myles handed Fleurentine's journal back to Lance. "You got all that just from looking at the genealogical chart?"

"It was the last piece of the puzzle." Lance held up the black book. "This journal isn't the only family archive out there. Most of my family is trying to conquer the future, but some of us are still wielding the past."

Back out on the street, Kendell hugged Myles's arm as they walked toward the river. "They're holding all the cards, aren't they?"

"What do you mean?"

"The baron handed his ledgers down through the Laroque family, thus giving them the money and influence to achieve their goals to this day. Antoine probably handed what information he had about his father and the curse to another of his children in an attempt to keep the Laroques in check. Then he buried the cursed items in the walls of the homes he built to keep them from causing harm. Even if we did have some evidence Marilyn was murdered, what would we do with it? Go up against the New Orleans chief of police? Notify the FBI? We couldn't even use it for political purposes without being laughed at. We've lost. All we have is this stupid pipe tool, and if we hang onto it, we'll just be in more danger."

He took her hand. "What were we trying to win? We proved I can read an object's energy. That's huge, in my opinion, even if it's just the two of us who know it. I finally have someone who believes in me. We've got a pretty good idea of where you fit into the families of New Orleans. We may not have proof of anything that's going on, but that's not a bad thing. People who know too much end up in danger. We have some connections to the paranormal world. And though I don't like the guy, Lance gave us one emergency card. Whether or not the items Fleurentine left at the convent are cursed, the Laroque family knows we have access to them. Hopefully, that threat will be enough to keep them off our backs."

"Or they could force us to retrieve them."

Myles pointed at the imposing modern structure next to the ferry terminal. "I think it's time we got rid of the pipe tool and secured what little support may be available. From what Lieutenant Cazenave said, whatever agency resides in the abandoned World Trade Center may be the only official entity in New Orleans willing to listen."

Kendell stared at the ground. He knew she was avoiding eye contact, and that was never a good thing. "There's something I've been keeping from you. Ever since we shared our spirits, I've had this rush of energy when I'm around the cursed tool. Something happened to me that day. I didn't tell you because I didn't want you thinking you'd somehow damaged me. It wasn't your fault."

Her explanation sound too much like the familiar *It's not you, it's me* brush-off he'd heard from past girlfriends. "Then why do I suddenly feel like it is my doing?"

She pulled his hand into the pocket of her coat, though whether the move was for warmth or to have him physically close, he couldn't tell. He felt the pipe tool nestled in the bottom. "I only have one metaphor for what I'm feeling, but please don't read too much into it. When a girl loses her virginity, assuming the act is consensual, she doesn't blame the boy. This energy I feel reminds me of that first time. Suddenly, I felt connected to everyone around me like a barrier had been lowered. What you did for me was open me up to all this life force that's constantly around all of us."

He was beginning to understand. "And that tool is filled with a dark energy you can no longer prevent from consuming you."

"I wouldn't go that far. I can't control it. That frightens me. But that power also excites the hell out of me. You saw me that night on stage. That rush could too easily become an addiction. I know we have to get rid of it. Just like a drunk knows he needs to pour the bottle of whisky down the drain."

19

*M*yles stared up at the thirty-three-story abandoned World Trade Center. "We're doing the right thing. Aren't we?" The traffic and pedestrians at the foot of Canal Street made the empty building look all the more ominous in its neglected 1960s glory.

"It's too dangerous for either of us to keep the pipe tool. Lieutenant Cazenave said it would be safe here."

He hated the idea of her having the cursed item in her apartment. Someone would always be after it. "You realize his boss's boss is Chief of Police Laroque. We may be giving that family exactly what they want."

"If the chief knew about it, I don't think we would have made it out of the police station. I think Lieutenant Cazenave uses the lack of respect he gets from his fellow officers to conduct his real work in private. After all, he had us bring the pipe tool here and not to the police station."

Myles didn't like anything about the situation. Walking into an abandoned building carrying a cursed object that the most powerful family in New Orleans wanted and likely used for killing didn't seem like a smart move. But then, holding onto the damn thing wasn't any better. "I would say I should go alone. There's no point in both of us walking into danger. But you'd just tell me to stuff it, so I won't."

She took his hand and started walking across the grass that separated the sidewalk from the front entrance. "Nice to see you're learning. I let Polly and the girls know what we're up to just in case something goes wrong."

The floor-to-ceiling glass windows were covered with aging drapes. Only the front entry had been left open. After the buzzer proved useless, it took a couple of hard knocks to get the security guard to look up from his novel. Myles suspected he might have been sleeping, though he couldn't imagine who would care about how the elderly man in the blue uniform filled his time. Even from outside, Myles could hear the man's hard-soled shoes scuffing along the dusty tile floor. The old guard didn't seem in any hurry. Once he'd traversed the distance from the desk to the door, he fumbled through the keys on his belt to finally unlock the door. "We're not open."

Kendell presented the business card the Lieutenant had given her with the symbol on the back. "Joseph Cazenave sent us."

The man nodded and pointed toward the row of elevators. "Take the middle one to the twenty-fourth floor. I'll let them know you're coming."

The elevator wasn't nearly as dirty or run-down as

Myles had expected, though that did little to ease his apprehension of what they would encounter when the doors opened. The Lieutenant had been a reasonable man at the police station. Myles tried to envision the most likely scenario. Even if they were handing the pipe tool off to the wrong people, the meeting would be a short, polite exchange, and then they'd be ushered out of the building. The last thing the secretive agency would want would be for questions to arise about the missing couple. But using intellect to argue they would be safe did little to calm his beating heart. Once again, he was walking Kendell into a dangerous situation.

When the doors opened, he was surprised to see a receptionist sitting at the desk of a well-lit, nicely decorated office. "He's expecting you. You can go on in."

Unlike what Myles had seen of the rest of the building, the wood-paneled office lined with shelves filled with dusty books more aptly resembled his grandfather's den than a modern business office. All the heavyset gentleman in the tweed jacket needed was a cigar to complete the image. "Joseph mentioned you might be stopping by. Please have a seat."

Kendell ran her hand along the book spines as she read the titles. "What is this place?"

"A repository of the paranormal."

Myles sat in the overstuffed leather chair. He wondered how much of the office was intentionally designed to put guests at ease. The feeling of being manipulated kept him on edge, but at least his initial fears of being threatened hadn't materialized. "Lieutenant Cazenave said our pipe tool would be kept safe here. What are you willing to tell us about what you do?"

The man's high-backed chair creaked as he leaned back. "You're hesitant. I get that a lot. You've stumbled across the Malveaux curse, and unless I'm much mistaken—which doesn't happen often—I'd say you were ready to be rid of that murderous knife. Let me start off by explaining where you are. Have you ever wondered why this building is so different from the rest of the structures around it?"

Modern architecture had never really interested Myles. "I guess a big X-shaped footprint is kind of odd."

The man's laugh, like the office, was pitched at just the right depth to put Myles at ease. "It's not odd. From any reasonable assessment, it's the most foolish design possible for surviving a hurricane. Instead of shedding the wind and rain like a triangle or circle, or even a well-positioned square, this thing catches any storm headed this way. Officially, it was built to house offices for international operations looking to do business in New Orleans."

The history lesson was beginning to grow boring.

"Like most people, I assume I lost you at the word 'international.' That too was intentional. The real purpose is to house dangerous artifacts. Think of our possessions like nuclear waste. The only thing worse than having one barrel of the stuff is to have hundreds of barrels all stacked together. To keep the energy from building to unsafe levels, the stuff needs to be kept isolated. That's where the design of this building comes into play. By having four wings on every floor, our objects can be kept secure from each other. The wind that whips down the inner angles of the structure further ensures such power doesn't accumulate."

Kendell turned from her inspection of the books. "So this was never an office building?"

"We did house offices for a time. Our occupants helped with the cover story. But once Hurricane Katrina hit, we were able to claim the building unsafe. Which it is, just not structurally. This place is built stronger than most bomb shelters."

Myles didn't see much reason to continue pussyfooting around his big question. "Who are you? Are you with the government?"

"My name is Luther Noire. Governments are too temporary. There's a reason this is the *World* Trade Center. As a way of explaining this organization, I'd like you to imagine something. See yourself as an early caveman. You're squatting over a boulder with a rock in your hand. By slamming the rock against a nut that's on the boulder, you're able to crack the shell and get at the meat. Now another caveman comes along, but instead of just having a rock, he's tied his to the end of a stick. With the increased force, he's able to smash the nut with far less effort. You might see such a person as having mystical skills and the hammer he's formed as being supernatural, which from your experience it would be. Such a tool could be dangerous in the wrong hands."

Kendell put her hand on Myles's shoulder. "So your organization is international and pre-dates our modern understanding of governments. That could only mean the church."

230

"A very good guess but not accurate. We're more of an offshoot of many religions. The Catholics, for example, are happy to contain what they consider their holy relics. Their means of keeping such items safe is to instruct their congregations to worship the items. But not all objects can be traced to saints. That's where we come in. We take the castoffs."

Kendell pulled the pipe tool from her pocket and set it on the desk. "Like this?"

Instead of picking up the cylinder Mr. Noire opened a ledger that took up half of his desk. He pulled some spectacles out of the pocket of his jacket that looked as old as the pipe tool. The small lime-green lenses looked out of proportion on his large face. Myles realized he'd seen the color before in the glasses Lieutenant Cazenave had worn at the police station, but he'd discounted the eerie tint as being a reflection of the tile walls.

Mr. Noire's eyes were enlarged to the size of the lenses. "I need you both to tell me your story. Start as far back as you can. Don't try to make a long story short. I want it all. And rest assured that I can see the truth."

What amazed Myles about the telling of their adventure was how smoothly he and Kendell handed off the narrative. Like a play where the dialogue had been well rehearsed, not once did they contradict each other. She even helped with his explanation of his psychometric abilities. He grasped her hand at her insight on their shared consciousness exploring the pipe tool's original curse. She handled the experience of him as a small boy with great sensitivity, and she didn't shy away from his connection to her as a young girl. Mr. Noire diligently recorded the pertinent information in his elegantly cursive handwriting.

Once Mr. Noire had the story fully recorded, he turned his attention to the pipe tool. "Such an ordinary little item." He made a production of wrapping the tool in cellophane, then wrapping it again in velvet, and finally setting it in a rough-hewn wooden box lined with some kind of metal.

"What happens to the pipe tool now?" Kendell asked.

"With any luck, it and the events surrounding it will be forgotten. People have an amazing ability to ignore things they don't understand. The church believes by putting their superstitions on display, that power will either be considered antiquated and foolish or revered and holy. But they have the luxury of focusing on their relics' abilities to do good. Parishioners are told the object has more power than any individual should handle. Dealing with cursed items is more like keeping the cookie jar on the top shelf so children can't get to it. The power to do evil is always more tempting than to do good."

Myles considered Mr. Noire's explanation naïve. "What about the Laroque family? They're not likely to just forget about the curse."

"The curse, no. But this pipe tool is already listed as missing from the police evidence room. I count my successes one item at a time."

Myles still had more questions than answers. "You don't worry about that putting Lieutenant Cazenave in danger of being discovered as your mole in the department?"

Mr. Noire removed his glasses and settled back in his chair. "Danger is all around us every day. By standing on the front line of good versus evil, we ensure the general public is free to carry on with their daily lives—just as you two should do."

It wasn't until Myles was back out on the street that Kendell articulated the thought that had been bugging him. "Do you think he meant we should get on with our lives like everyone else, or we're supposed to be standing with him on the front line?"

"I think he intended it to be a question we had to ask ourselves. You do realize that pipe tool isn't the only object under the Malveaux curse?"

The street was filled with children headed to the aquarium for a school outing. She took a seat on one of the metal benches and watched the procession. "You're worried each of those items might find its way to me. I can't run away. I know that was my mom's decision, but it's not mine. She couldn't have known the current dangers. Even though the family stories would have sounded like just superstitious nonsense, in her heart she would have felt a need to leave. I think I understand her just a little bit better now."

His heart leapt at the idea of her staying. Their connection had been forged by the combination of danger, mutual acceptance, and trust. "I want to make sure you know what you're saying. We'll be going up against one of the most powerful families in the country."

She smiled at him for some time before answering. "Does that mean you're staying too?"

She'd caught his unintended admission of emotion, but his feelings weren't necessarily something he wanted to keep hidden. "We're more than partners. If you're staying, I'll be right here beside you."

~

AFTER A WEEK of being free of the cursed tool, Kendell began to feel like her old self. It wasn't a feeling she liked. Even doubling up on her coffee intake had only made her nervous without providing the adrenaline rush she craved.

She sat at the outdoor café, fidgeting. She was intentionally early. The prospect of arriving to see Myles already seated with her mother had been avoided, but as a result, she had to sit and wait. At least she had Cheesecake to keep her company. "Why am I so nervous, girl? It's not like I care what my mother thinks."

Cheesecake looked up with her deep, soulful eyes as if to ask the question Kendell had felt growing in her heart since the night Myles had come to their rescue.

"It doesn't matter what I say to you, does it? You see right through me."

Cheesecake snuggled close to her leg and lifted her shaggy head to Kendell's knee.

Kendell petted the floppy ears. "I know you're always on my side."

"What are you two up to?" They both smiled to see Myles arrive.

"Just waiting on you. I guess I was a little early. Cheesecake pulled me the whole way."

He sat next to her with Cheesecake at their feet. "It's just lunch. Some women do find me quite charming, you know.

I'm sure I can carry on a conversation with your mother without unduly embarrassing you."

Ever since their shared mental connection into the tool's energy, he'd been able to read her a little too well for her comfort. Not that she couldn't also tell what he was feeling. "Maybe it's not her impression I'm worried about."

"Since you know me better than to worry what I think, I'll have to conclude you're somehow worried about how Cheesecake will view our interaction." He reached down and ran his fingernails along the dog's spine, which caused her to arch her back with enjoyment.

"You're even getting to know my dog too well."

"Seriously, though, I know you followed me down this paranormal rabbit hole. If we hadn't tried to figure out my abilities, we never would have bought that pipe tool in the first place. I put you both in danger. Your mother would have every right to think I was a bad influence on you."

For someone who understood her so well, he could still revert to that stupid male mentality without much effort. "You know that's not the way I see it. I talked you into every step of this journey."

Before he could attempt another lame-ass response, she saw her mother approaching the table. Kendell barely got a hug in before her mother bent down to greet Cheesecake. "How's the pretty girl? Who's a good girl? Is it you?"

Cheesecake endured the childish actions of the older woman with the reserve she always showed to those of lesser dignity. Kendell, however, still found her mother's antics when it came to dogs embarrassing. "Mom, I'd like you to meet Myles."

She felt bad for him. Like Cheesecake, Myles attempted a classier approach than her mother. He held out his hand only to be embraced in a full-body bear hug. Kendell wouldn't have felt as bad if her mother had at least worn a bra under the lightweight tie-dyed dress. "It's so good to finally meet the man who entices my daughter out of her shell."

For a moment, Kendell wondered if she could eat her lunch under the table with Cheesecake. Myles took her hand. "I suspect you underestimate her. I've never met a more confident woman."

"We're talking about my daughter? The one constantly hiding in the overcoat?"

Myles gave Kendell an appraising smile. "Just like a superhero. Only those that truly know her recognize the strength within."

Kendell sat and listened to the two debate her character. Her mother's representation was of a young girl hiding in her room playing her guitar and avoiding any form of social interaction. She recognized the loner in her mother's narrative, but she'd outgrown that phase long ago. Myles, however, spoke of a woman who was fearless. In his eyes, she was a heroine devoted to protecting others and searching out the truth.

She suspected neither characterization was completely accurate. Vestiges of her mother's description still crept up far too often. And though the events she'd shared with Myles had to be the basis for his assessment, that courageous woman he saw in her was still often a front for her insecurities. By the end of the meal, she realized her initial fear hadn't been for her mother's and Myles's assessment of each other. It was for her personal impression.

Back out on the path that ran along the levee, he held her hand. "Do you want to talk about whatever it is that's really bothering you? Because I don't believe it has anything to do with me meeting your mother."

She knew it was pointless to try and hide anything from him. "Ever since we turned the pipe tool over to Mr. Noire, I've had this emptiness inside. At first I thought it was a lack of purpose. I was playing an important role in keeping the Malveaux curse from doing harm. But as the days passed, I realized there was more to it. I'd grown addicted to that energy, dark as it was. It flowed through me like caffeine, heightening my senses and relentlessly driving me forward. Even that longing for power I could deal with, though. My biggest fear is that I've lost the self-confidence you told my mother about. What if what you know about me is really nothing more than some curse-induced bravado? What happens when you find out I'm not as strong as you think I am?"

He stopped walking and turned her to face him. "I knew you before we found the tool. I've walked beside you every step in this adventure. And I know you now. We all go through changes. I promise you. There's nothing for you to worry about. You are an amazing person. We all find people, events, and even dogs that give us strength and make us who we want to be. At best, things only magnify what's already there. Objects don't change us."

She felt the confidence building in her chest to conquer

the hardest challenge of all. "I've trusted you with my life, with my dog—and if you'll let me—with my heart."

As he let go of her hands, she feared her strength would disappear into the rushing river. Instead, he wrapped his arms around her waist and lifted her to his mouth for the kiss she had doubted would ever come. Her emotions melted into his as she pressed her body hard against him. Her arms were so tight around his neck she feared she'd strangle him.

Cheesecake jumped and barked with glee around them —wrapping them tightly together with her leash.

BOOK LIST

Writing as G.A. Chase

The Malveaux Curse Series:

Dog Days of Voodoo

You Me and The Voodoo Queen (coming soon)

Oops! I Voodoo'd Again (coming soon)

Writing as Greg Chase

Technopia Series:

Creation

Evolution

Damnation

Salvation

ABOUT THE AUTHOR

G.A. Chase is the pen name for Greg Chase. He has previously written as a science fiction author and is a glass artist living in New Orleans with his wife, fellow author Deanna Chase, and their two shih tzu dogs. On any given day you can find him behind his computer, people watching in the quarter, or out in his studio creating stories in glass. His glass work can be found at www.chase-designs.com.

For more information
www.gregchaseauthor.com